"Why a... at me...

Samantha asked softly.

"I'm trying to understand what it is I feel when I'm with you. I want to take you off someplace where we can be alone."

A smile touched her mouth. "What you're feeling is called lust."

Pierce's finger brushed her mouth. "I want to kiss you here." His hand trailed over her cheek and down her neck. "And here." It moved inside the collar of her blouse and slowly down. "And here."

Samantha's imagination traveled right along with him. "Pierce."

"Umm."

"I don't think we should do this. People are watching."

"Let them."

"You don't mean that."

"You're right." Samantha sighed.

"What's the matter?"

"I was half hoping I was wrong."

Dear Reader:

In May of 1980 Silhouette had a goal. We wanted to bring you the best that romance had to offer—heartwarming, poignant stories that would move you time and time again.

Mission impossible? Not likely, because in 1980 and all the way through to today, we have authors with the same dream we have—writers who strive to bring you stories with a distinctive medley of charm, wit, and above all, *romance*.

And this fall we're celebrating in the Silhouette Romance line—we're having a Homecoming! In September some of your all-time favorite authors are returning to their "alma mater." Then, during October, we're honored to present authors whose books always capture the magic—some of the wonderful writers who have helped maintain the heartwarming quality the Silhouette Romance line is famous for.

Come home to Romance this fall and for always. Help celebrate the special world of Silhouette Romance.

I hope you enjoy this book and the many books to come.

Sincerely,

Tara Hughes
Senior Editor
Silhouette Books

BRITTANY YOUNG

Far from Over

Silhouette Romance

Published by Silhouette Books New York

America's Publisher of Contemporary Romance

SILHOUETTE BOOKS
300 E. 42nd St., New York, N.Y. 10017

Copyright © 1987 by Brittany Young

ISBN: 0-373-08537-0

First Silhouette Books printing October 1987

America's Publisher of Contemporary Romance

Printed in the U.S.A.

BRITTANY YOUNG

lives and writes in Racine, Wisconsin. She has traveled to most of the countries that serve as the settings for her Romances and finds the research into the language, customs, history and literature of these countries among the most demanding and rewarding aspects of her writing.

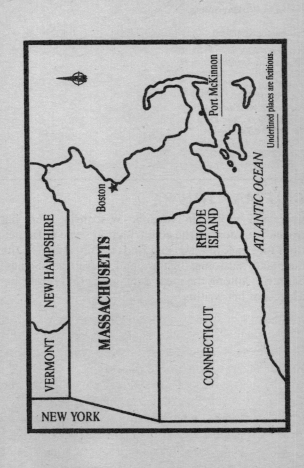

VERMONT

NEW HAMPSHIRE

NEW YORK

MASSACHUSETTS

Boston

CONNECTICUT

RHODE ISLAND

Port McKinnon

ATLANTIC OCEAN

Underlined places are fictitious.

Chapter One

Samantha English stood as inconspicuously as she could at two o'clock in the morning on the Boston street, and stared at the front door of a quaint but elegant hotel. She looked at her watch and decided to give it another half hour and then pack it up.

A couple walked past her, their arms around each other, their heads together, talking quietly. A soft smile curved Samantha's mouth as she watched them. The sultry summer night was perfect for lovers. There was a romantic hush about things.

A light breeze blew, lifting her heavy red hair and cooling the back of her neck and her temples. The worst part of being a detective was the waiting. She was always waiting for someone else to do something.

Suddenly the hotel door opened, and a man in his thirties walked out and stood still for a moment while lighting a cigarette. It was Albert von Schmidt. Samantha's heart beat a little faster. This was the same thing he'd done last night and the night before. And if he continued to follow his pattern, he'd be gone on his walk for forty minutes—plenty of time for her to search his hotel room. Though what she expected to find, heaven only knew. She certainly didn't. Just something out of place.

The man strolled away from her, but Samantha stayed where she was until several minutes after he was out of sight. Then she moved quickly toward the building and went into the nearly deserted lobby as though she owned the place. She'd learned a long time ago not to appear self-conscious when she was doing something she shouldn't. But despite that attitude, her heart was pounding. Samantha wasn't a naturally sneaky person. She really had to work at it. This was an awful way to gather information for a client, and breaking and entering wasn't something she did lightly. She didn't even want to think about what might happen to her and her detective's license if she ever got caught. But until someone could come up with something better, this was the way it had to be.

As she moved through the lobby, Sam glanced casually around to see if anyone was watching. No one was. She breathed a little easier as she walked into an open elevator and pushed the button for the fifth floor. The doors slid closed with a soft thud and the old elevator, a stranger to the modern technology that made elevators faster than the speed of light, quietly started its well-oiled ascent. Sam put her hand on a wooden rail that ran the circumference of the elevator. Her short, well-tended nails nervously drummed as her eyes remained glued to the floor directory. First floor, second floor, third floor, fourth floor, fifth floor. The elevator stopped and the doors opened. She put her finger on the Hold button as she leaned out to examine the hall. It was deserted. She stealthily made her way down the plushly carpeted hallway to room 519.

Stopping, she again looked both ways down the empty hall before removing a palm-sized leather case from her purse, unzipping it and selecting the right size metal lock pick. Pushing her wavy red hair behind her ears, she bent over the door lock and inserted the pick. It made a little clicking noise, and she smiled with satisfaction when she felt the lock open. As she started to remove the pick, the door opened from the other side and Samantha found herself staring at a massive pajama-covered stomach.

With a sinking heart she straightened, her eyes moving up button by button to the man's neck, bearded chin, mouth, nose and eyes. She flashed him her most disarming smile. "Hi, there. I bet you're wondering..."

Samantha sat on the edge of a desk in the police station with a phone pressed against her ear, waiting for her secretary to answer. "Come on, Harriet," she muttered into the mouthpiece.

At last there was a click, and a sleepy voice said, "English Detective Agency. If it's lost, we'll find it."

"Hello, Harriet. You're supposed to be off duty."

There was a pause. "Samantha? What time is it?"

"Three o'clock in the morning."

"Why are you calling me at such a ridiculous hour?"

"Two reasons. The first one is to fire you. The second is to tell you to get in touch with my attorney."

The firing part went right over the secretary's head. She'd heard it too many times to believe it anymore. Samantha fired Harriet at least twice a week. "You need Mr. White at this hour of the morning? Why?"

"Why? Funny you should ask that, Harriet. It seems I've been arrested and I need him to get me out of jail."

"Jail?" Harriet sounded considerably more awake. "What are you doing there?"

"Yet another pertinent question, Harriet. I got caught breaking into a hotel room. The *wrong* hotel room, incidentally. The wrong room, yet the right room as far as the note you gave me goes."

"What one did I tell you was his?"

"Five-one-nine."

"Five-one-nine? Oh, no. It was five-nine-one. I'm quite sure."

"Five-nine-one?" Samantha pulled the slip of paper out of her pocket and looked at it again. It said very clearly 519.

"Yes. I remember because that was the exact amount I paid for my new chair. It's a wonderful chair. Did I show it to you?"

Samantha closed her eyes and forced herself to be patient. "No, but you've described it to me several times, Harriet."

"It's vinyl. Leather costs too much."

"Harriet?"

"Yes?"

"Call Mr. White, please."

"Right away." There was a pause. "I transposed the numbers again, didn't I?"

"Yes, Harriet."

"Sorry."

"I know."

"I'll call Mr. White now."

"Thank you." Samantha hung up and put her hands flat on the top of the desk as she swung her shapely legs back and forth.

"Hi, Sam."

She smiled at a policeman she knew as he walked by and then sighed. A whole night wasted because of a wrong room number. That same policeman came back a little later and handed her a cup of coffee. "Thought that might perk you up," he told her as he took the seat across from her.

"Thanks, Jack."

"I feel really bad about having to bring you in the way I did. Sorry."

"It's not your fault. I was the one who got caught."

"Do you mind if I ask what you were doing breaking in there?"

"Don't answer that."

Samantha turned at the sound of a deep voice and looked at the man standing behind her. He was in his thirties, very tall and dignified-looking with dark blond hair in a businessman's cut and dark brown eyes. The black tuxedo he had on fit his strong body as though it had been specially tailored. "I beg your pardon?"

"I said don't answer that."

"Why not?"

"Because, assuming you've been read your rights, whatever you say to this officer can be used in a court of law against you."

"But Jack wouldn't—"

"Never assume anything, Miss English."

Samantha studied the newcomer curiously. "Pardon me for asking, but precisely how does my predicament concern you?"

"I'm your attorney."

Samantha's gaze started at the man's head, traveled down to his toes and then came back up. "My attorney is overweight, slightly bald and sixty-two. You don't look a thing like him."

"Your attorney is out of town. When your secretary couldn't get in touch with him, she called my grandmother."

"Your grandmother?"

"Olivia Westcott."

Sam had apprenticed for a year under an old fellow before opening her own office. As he'd gradually phased out his business, he'd referred some of his clients to her. Olivia Westcott, a Vanderbilt-style matriarch, had been one of them. Before hiring someone new to work inside or on the grounds of her home, she had their backgrounds investigated. And that was how Sam had met her. They'd taken an instant liking to one another. Olivia, as she'd asked Samantha to call her, had even come from her home in Port McKinnon to have lunch with her a few times.

"That's right. I'm Pierce Westcott. Olivia asked me to help you out."

"I see." Sam motioned toward his tuxedo with a wave of her hand. "And you were obviously out for the evening. I'm sorry to be such a bother."

He ignored her apology as if she'd never made it, and turned his attention to the policeman. "If you don't mind, Officer, I'd like to speak with my client."

The officer rose. "Of course. Later, Sam."

Pierce lowered himself into the seat the man vacated, leaned comfortably back and watched Samantha for an unnerving ninety seconds before speaking. "I know what the police say happened, but I want to hear your version."

"My *version*?"

He lifted his eyebrow expressively. "Does my choice of words offend you?"

She found his attitude more than a little annoying. "I thought my tone of voice made that quite clear."

He just continued looking at her. "Miss English, I frankly don't care if you spend the rest of your natural life in jail. But my grandmother obviously has a fondness for you, and I don't want her worried. I'm here strictly as a favor to her. Nothing more and nothing less."

"And you're doing it so graciously, too, Mr. Westcott. Perhaps you feel I should save the courts money and simply go straight to jail like a good little girl."

"From what I was told when I arrived, jail is exactly where you belong."

"Well, thank you for your opinion and now, if you don't mind, I think I'll get another attorney. One less ready to hang me before he hears my side of it."

"Miss English, my opinion of people of your ilk has nothing to do with my ability to represent you."

Samantha actually felt her blood pressure rise. "My ilk?" she said with masterful restraint. "Now I'm a member of an ilk? Can you tell from the tone of my voice this time that I'm offended, Mr. Westcott? Because if not, I should tell you that I'm offended. In fact, I'm furious. You sit there in all of your pretentious pomposity..." Samantha paused. "Pretentious pomposity," she said thoughtfully. "I like that. But I digress. How dare you. How *dare* you make judgments on my integrity..."

"Or lack thereof," he suggested. "I mean, you were arrested breaking into a man's hotel room."

Samantha withered him with a look. She had to because she couldn't think of a single thing to say in her defense.

"What's the matter, Miss English? Does the truth hurt?"

Her eyes met his for a quiet moment. "Yours does," she admitted softly. "I suppose I do look like that through your eyes."

Her complete turnabout took Pierce off guard, and he looked at her in curious surprise. "It doesn't matter how you look through my eyes, Miss English. What matters is how you look through the district attorney's eyes." When his grandmother had told him about Samantha earlier in the evening, he'd created a picture in his mind that wasn't anything like the woman before him. Detectives weren't very high on his list of preferred professions. So many of them were sleazy, disreputable types, bleeding clients of their money while providing very little service. But this woman wasn't like that. He could tell just by looking at her. Her gaze was open and intelligent. This was a woman who would have a difficult time lying to any-one. Pierce's conscience didn't often bother him, but it did now. "I'm sorry, Miss English. That was un-called-for."

Now it was Samantha's turn to be surprised. "Thank you."

A corner of Pierce's mouth lifted. "There's no need to look at me like that."

"I'm sorry, but you just don't look like the kind of man who apologizes often."

"I'm not. And now if we can get on with this, I'd like you to tell me what happened tonight."

Samantha met his look with a direct one of her own as she pushed her heavy hair away from her face. "You can't imagine how embarrassing this is."

"There's no reason to feel that way, Miss English. How bad can it be?"

She laughed. "Pretty bad. And do you think we could use first names? I'd be more comfortable using Pierce and Samantha."

"That's fine."

"Thank you." There was just the slightest pause. "I'll be Samantha."

The grooves in Pierce's cheeks deepened, making him even more attractive. She got the distinct feeling that he didn't smile very often. "Stop stalling."

Sam took a deep breath, gathering her courage. "As you already know, I tried to break into a hotel room."

"Why?"

Samantha looked at him blankly. *"Why?"*

"If the questions get too tough, let me know."

"There's no need for sarcasm. It just struck me as being an odd thing to ask. What does it matter *why* I was breaking in? The act is what was illegal, no matter what the motivation."

Pierce studied her in disconcerting silence. "I'm not the enemy, Samantha. I'm trying to help you. Now tell me why you were breaking into that hotel room."

"I'm sorry," she apologized. "I'm not trying to be difficult. Really. It's just that I can't tell you."

"Why?" Then Pierce answered his own question. "Ah, yes, detective-client confidentiality." His eyes rested on her for a long moment. She was one of the loveliest women he'd ever seen. There was a dimple at the corner of her mouth that deepened charmingly with very little provocation. Pierce leaned toward her. "Samantha, if you don't tell me what went on," he explained patiently, "I can't defend you."

Samantha slid off the desk and walked away from him.

"I won't repeat what you tell me. My business with you is just as confidential as your business with your client."

"It's not that," she said quietly.

"Then what is it?"

"I already told you. It's embarrassing."

"Swallow your pride."

She turned and looked at him again. "That's easy for you to say." Then she sighed. "All right. Consider it swallowed. I have a client who's in some trouble, and he feels the occupant of a room in that hotel has information that could straighten everything out."

"In the room you tried to break into?"

"Ah, well, that's the embarrassing part."

"I don't understand."

"It was the wrong room," she mumbled.

"Excuse me?"

Samantha flashed him a look of exasperation. "It was the wrong room," she enunciated more clearly.

Pierce somehow managed not to laugh, but he couldn't keep his mouth from twitching. "I see."

"I thought you might."

At that, Pierce allowed himself to smile. "If you don't mind my asking, how did you happen to break into the wrong room?"

"My secretary transposed the room number."

"I hope you fired her."

"I fire her regularly. But this time I'm going to have a serious talk with her."

"I imagine she's quaking in her high heels."

Samantha's dimple flashed. "All right. I admit it. I'm not the toughest boss in the world."

Brown eyes looked into blue. Pierce's gaze roamed over Samantha's face. She had the most wonderful smile.

Samantha felt suddenly self-conscious. "What's wrong?"

A corner of his mouth lifted. "Why do you automatically assume that there's something wrong when someone's looking at you?"

"Not 'someone.' You."

"A paranoid detective. What a combination." He studied her curiously. "You look like a woman who could be anything she wanted. Tell me, Samantha English, what are you doing in Boston playing detective?"

"Don't be patronizing," she said good-naturedly. "I'm not *playing* detective. It's what I do for a living."

"But why?"

"Why not?"

"One of the first rules of conversation is that you're not supposed to answer a question with another question."

"Strange, the things you learn when you least expect it."

"Wouldn't you rather be doing something where you could earn a decent living?"

"I'm hardly living in poverty. I've only been in business for six months and things are picking up nicely."

"You still haven't answered the big 'why' question."

"Why am I a detective?" She lifted her shoulders. "I guess I've just gotta be me." Sam looked thoughtfully into the distance. "I seem to feel a song coming on."

Pierce laughed, surprising himself as much as Sam.

Her eyes rested on him. "You have a nice laugh. You should use it more often."

"What makes you think I don't?"

"Your grandmother. She talks about you sometimes."

"And what does she say?"

"That you've been the head of the Westcott household since you were only twenty-one. That you've raised two sisters and one brother. That you brought your family from the brink of financial ruin back to being one of the most powerful families in the country. You haven't exactly had a lot of time for laughter."

"My grandmother talks too much."

"Of course, she didn't tell me all I know about you."

"Oh? Are you clairvoyant?"

Sam shook her head. "Nothing so glamorous. I'm just Samantha English, intuitive detective."

"Detective." Pierce's voice reflected his distaste.

Samantha just looked at him.

"Uh-oh. My tone again?"

"I wasn't going to say anything. You apparently can't help yourself." Samantha looked around the surprisingly busy station and sighed tiredly. "Do I have to spend the night in jail?"

Pierce said nothing. His mind seemed to be elsewhere, though his eyes were on her.

"Pierce?"

"Yes?"

"I asked if I had to spend the night in jail."

"Oh. No. I've already posted bail."

"You mean that I can go home?"

"I mean we both can."

Samantha's eyes rested on his. "Thank you."

"You're welcome." He held out his hand to help her down from the desk. "Come on, Sherlock. Let's get out of here."

As they walked through the old halls of the police station, Sam gave Pierce a very thorough once-over out of the corner of her eye. He seemed older than his years. Older and very reserved. She didn't hold that against him, though. What she knew of him, she had to respect.

They stepped into the cool night and stopped walking. Samantha took a deep breath to clear away the stuffiness of the police station.

"Where's your car?"

"At the hotel where I was arrested."

"I'll give you a ride to it."

"I hate to put you to any more trouble than I already have."

"It's no trouble. I have to go in that direction anyway." He put his hand under her elbow and led her to a black Jaguar sedan across the street. A woman was already in the front seat, so Pierce opened the rear door and Sam climbed in.

"Hi," she said with a smile at the woman. "I'm Samantha English."

The woman reached between the front seats and shook her hand. "Barbara Lowell."

Barbara was stunning, with short, sculpted blond hair and finely drawn aristocratic features. Samantha couldn't have picked a more perfect female complement to Pierce. "I apologize for all the problems I've caused this evening."

"That's all right," Barbara said graciously. "We were getting ready to leave the party anyway."

Pierce folded his long legs behind the steering wheel, put the car into gear and pulled into the empty street. Barbara stretched her arm out so that her hand rested lightly on Pierce's shoulder. "Where are we going now?"

"Samantha left her car a few miles away from here."

"Oh." Barbara turned her head and studied Samantha. "If I'm not being too nosy, what exactly were you arrested for?"

Samantha started to answer, but Pierce did it for her. "It's nothing more than a little misunderstanding that'll be straightened out in a day or two."

"I'm so glad. I presume it was in the line of duty."

"Line of duty?" Samantha asked.

"Pierce told me on the way over here that you're a private detective."

"Oh, that."

"Rather an unusual profession for a woman."

"Not really."

"I guess what I'm saying is that when I heard you were a private investigator, I was expecting you to be some bruising hulk of a woman. But you're so...so..."

Pierce's eyes went to the rearview mirror and looked at Samantha. "Delicate," Pierce finished for her.

Barbara looked over at him with a slightly arched eyebrow. "Exactly."

Samantha didn't say anything. She was so tired of the stereotypes that she didn't bother to defend herself anymore.

"Do you actually enjoy your work?" Barbara asked.

"I actually do, Barbara, yes. And what do you do for a living?" Samantha made a not-very-subtle attempt at changing the conversation.

"At the moment I'm involved in interior design, but mostly for friends. It's not really a business. I don't even charge a fee. Instead, I have my clients donate what they would ordinarily have paid a professional to the charity of my choice.''

"That's very noble of you.''

Barbara looked at her quickly to see if she was being sarcastic. Samantha smiled innocently back at her.

As Barbara spoke quietly to Pierce, Samantha relaxed in her seat and watched the two of them. Well, mostly Pierce. His shoulders were broad, even in the tuxedo. He seemed very athletic. She suddenly felt compelled to look in the rearview mirror, and found Pierce watching her watch him. But instead of looking away, she held his gaze. There were unplumbed depths to this man. She could see it in his eyes. He was the kind of man you could know for a lifetime and yet not really know at all. An interesting kind of man, and yet a little frightening. They drove for a while in silence until Barbara interrupted it. "I understand that your connection with the Westcott family is through Pierce's grandmother.''

"That's right.''

"Then you must be invited to Pierce's sister's wedding on Saturday. Are you coming?''

Olivia had sent her an invitation. "I hope so, yes.''

"It should be lovely," Barbara continued. "The wedding itself is going to be a small family affair at the Port McKinnon church, but the reception afterwards at the beach house is going to be huge.''

Samantha had to smile when Barbara referred to the Westcott's fifty-room mansion on the ocean as a beach house.

"Where is your car, Samantha?'' asked Pierce.

She focused on her surroundings and suddenly realized they were in front of the hotel. "Turn right at the corner."

He did.

"It's the yellow Jeep."

Pierce parked behind it and climbed out. Samantha turned back to Barbara. "I really am sorry about taking you away from the party, but I appreciate the rescue more than I can say. It was nice meeting you, Barbara."

"Nice meeting you, too, Samantha. I hope the rest of your evening is less eventful."

Pierce took her hand in his and helped her out of the car. Samantha stood on the pavement and looked at their joined hands for a moment, then slowly removed hers.

"What's wrong?"

She looked up at him, at a loss for words. Something was indeed wrong, but she couldn't honestly say that she knew what it was. She just knew she didn't want Pierce to touch her. Or was the problem that she did want him to touch her?

Pierce's eyes rested on her preoccupied profile as he walked her to the Jeep. "There's no need to look so worried. I have a feeling this whole thing can be resolved without a problem."

Samantha looked at him blankly. "Excuse me?"

"Your breaking and entering. What did you think I was talking about?"

"I'm sorry. My mind was obviously elsewhere." She was silent for a moment. "I could lose my license over something like this."

"That's not going to happen."

"How do you know?"

"Attorney's intuition."

Samantha smiled at the casual way he tossed her own words back at her. "You got me." She extended her hand as her eyes met his. "Thanks for showing up tonight. If it weren't for you, I'd still be in jail."

He took her hand in his, and Samantha was amazed at how aware of his touch she was, even in a simple handshake. "You don't have to thank me, Samantha."

"I know. I'll be billed." Her eyes twinkled.

But Pierce didn't smile. On the contrary. He seemed to be frowning at her.

Sam's own smile faded. "I should be going."

Pierce released her hand. "I feel as though I should follow you just to make sure you get home all right."

"I promise not to break into any more hotel rooms for at least a day."

Pierce still wasn't happy about her being out alone at this hour of the morning. He took a pen and a business card out of his pocket, scribbled something on the back of it and handed it to her. "I usually stay in my Boston home during the week. That's the phone number. If you need me, call."

"I will. Thank you."

"And I'll be talking to you in the morning. What time do you usually get to your office?"

"I work out of my home. But if I'm not there, just give my secretary, Harriet Fishbain, whatever message you have."

"Harriet Fishbain." The grooves in Pierce's cheeks deepened. "Only you could have a secretary with a name like that."

"And yours is probably named," she thought for a moment, "Smith . . . or Smythe."

"Smith. Frances Smith."

Their eyes locked. Pierce's smile faded slightly as he stared at her. "Good night, Samantha."

"Good night, Pierce."

They stood like that for a moment longer, staring at each other. Samantha suddenly realized what she was doing and broke the spell they had fallen under by turning away from Pierce and climbing into her Jeep.

Pierce went back to his own car, and Sam watched until his taillights were out of sight before starting her Jeep. But she didn't drive off right away. Instead she sat there, deep in thought. Not about what might happen tomorrow, which is what should have been on her mind. She was thinking about Pierce Westcott. There was something about him that was rock-solid and safe. But it was more than that.

There was a reserve about Pierce that distanced him from whomever he was with. She'd noticed it when he was in the police station with her and she'd noticed it later in the car with Barbara. Sam wondered if any woman had ever gotten beneath that dignified reserve—and she strongly doubted it. It was quite a challenge, and not one she'd ordinarily accept. But this was different. She didn't feel as though she'd just met him. She felt as though she'd known him for a long time. That she'd somehow been waiting for him without realizing it until she'd looked up at the police station and seen him standing there. What did it mean?

With a shake of her head, Sam made a U-turn on the semi-deserted city street and headed for home.

Chapter Two

Samantha lived in an old Victorian house that she had just finished remodeling. It was crowded in among other old homes and didn't have very much lawn, but she loved it.

She parked the Jeep in the narrow driveway and walked up the creaky wooden steps to the porch.

"Hello, Miss English," a voice said from beside her.

Samantha gasped and turned around, her hand over her heart, to face the little man who stood there. "Mr. Poondorken! You shouldn't sneak up on people like that!"

"Oh, gee, I'm sorry, Miss English." He had a voice similar to the nasal tones of the late Truman Capote.

"What are you doing here at this hour, anyway?"

"I wanted to ask if you found out anything. I mean, I don't know exactly what you were doing tonight, but you said you'd have some information for me in the morning. And, technically speaking, it *is* morning.''

Samantha looked at her watch. Four-thirty. ''Well, Mr. Poondorken, when you're right, you're right. How long have you been here?''

''Just a few hours.''

''Just a few hours.'' Samantha shook her head as she put her key in the lock and opened the heavy door. ''Come on in, Mr. Poondorken. Would you like some coffee?''

''No, thank you. A glass of milk sounds nice, though.''

''Milk. Of course.'' She tossed her purse and keys on the hall table and walked through the house to the kitchen, turning on lights as she went. Samantha took two glasses from an exposed shelf and set them on the island counter in the middle of the kitchen, then walked to the refrigerator while the little man sat on one of the chocolate-colored Gold Medal chairs. ''I'm afraid I don't really have any information for you. I had hoped to find something in von Schmidt's hotel room—''

''Von Schmidt's hotel room? How did you get in there?''

Samantha smiled wryly. ''Ah, there's the rub. I didn't.'' She poured him a glass of milk and then another for herself, and sat down next to him. ''Actually, I didn't get anywhere near it. I've spent all evening at the police station.''

''Why?''

''That's not important,'' she said quickly, not willing to embarrass herself any further. ''What I need is some more information from you, Mr. Poondorken.'' She paused at the sound of his name. ''May I call you Sidney?'' She couldn't say his last name without getting this incredible urge to smile. Fishbain and Poondorken. Where did she find these people?

''Certainly.''

''Thank you. As I was saying, I need more information. At the moment, all I know is that you were fired from your job for reasons which you claim to know nothing about, and that this Albert von Schmidt person is involved. What you've told me is very sketchy.''

''But I've told you everything I can.''

''Then I'm afraid I can't help you, Sidney. Even if I *had* been able to get into von Schmidt's hotel room, it wouldn't have done any good because I didn't really know what I was looking for. Just something out of place.''

''So you're off the case?''

''Unless you can be completely straight with me, you'll be doing nothing but wasting my time and your money.''

Sidney's upper teeth worked his lower lip. ''Then I guess I have no choice. I can't go back to that jail, and I won't go to prison for something I didn't do.''

''Back to jail?''

Sidney nodded. ''Remember what I told you about the company I worked for?''

''Only that it's called Amerigroup.''

''Right. Well, Amerigroup deals in high-tech research and development.''

''What was your role in the company?''

"I'm an engineer, and for the past eighteen months I've been in charge of the research-and-development laboratory."

She couldn't picture Sidney in charge of a department.

He pushed his glasses up on his nose. "And that's when the trouble started," he continued. "Only I didn't know it at the time."

"What trouble?"

Sidney tossed back the rest of his milk as if it was a shot of whiskey, then set the glass firmly on the counter. Samantha poured him another round. "They think I went bad."

"Went bad?"

"They believe I've been selling company secrets."

"You?" she asked in amazement.

A corner of his mouth lifted. "Not quite anyone's picture of an industrial spy, am I?"

"Certainly not mine. How did Amerigroup come to this incredible conclusion? No—" she lifted her hand to stop his answer "—we're getting ahead of ourselves. First, tell me what it is they think you stole."

"They don't know."

"They don't know?"

"They suspect it's a series of things, but they have no specific proof."

"Then how could they fire you? How could they have you arrested?"

"On suspicion."

"But why you?"

"Because I was the only one who didn't pass the lie-detector test."

Samantha sympathetically touched his hand. "Oh, Sidney."

"I was scared, Miss English. And the man who gave the test asked me such accusing questions. The needle started jumping from the moment he asked me whether or not my name was Sidney Poondorken."

She pushed her hair away from her face and leaned her elbows on the counter. "Why did they suspect you in the first place?"

Sidney reached into his pocket and pulled out several interest-bearing checking account balance sheets, which he put in front of her. Samantha picked them up and read the entries.

"Pay particular attention to the deposits, Miss English." He pointed out a few.

Several of them were for substantial sums of money—which most certainly couldn't have been accounted for by Sidney's legitimate earnings. "Where did you get this money?"

Sidney shook his head. "I don't know. But the dates of the deposits just happen to coincide with the completion time of certain projects which somehow managed to find their way into the hands of Amerigroup's competitors."

"Oh, no."

"Oh, yes."

"But how did it get into your account?"

"I don't know. I only know that I didn't put it there."

"Do you think it was computer tampering?"

"I did at first. It isn't all that hard to break into a bank's computer system. It just takes a little imagination and a lot of patience."

"Did you tell the bank?"

"Right away. But when they checked, they discovered that the money had indeed been deposited. So it obviously wasn't computer tampering."

"Sidney, are you saying that you actually have that much money in your account? That it isn't just a matter of someone playing with numbers?"

"That's exactly right. I couldn't believe it myself. I've been a fairly wealthy man, without knowing it, for months."

"You told the bank you hadn't made the deposits, didn't you?"

"Of course."

"What did they say?"

"Their own records were in order, so they figured I was some kind of nut. I didn't know what else to do, so I just let it ride, and reported it every time another deposit got recorded on my statements. I figured it was some kind of error on their part and eventually they'd discover it on their own." Sidney looked at Samantha, and there was fear in his eyes. "I did the right thing, didn't I? What else could I have done?"

Samantha smiled at him reassuringly. "Of course you did. I would have done the same thing myself. You had no idea the rest of this was going on. Besides, anyone who's ever dealt with a large company knows it's impossible to argue with a computer." She studied the statement a little longer, then placed it on the counter. "May I keep this?"

"Certainly, but I don't know what good it will do."

"Maybe none. We'll see." She thoughtfully tapped her nails on the counter. "Did anyone at Amerigroup mention who is suspected of paying you for information?''

"No. But I think that they think I'm going directly to the other companies involved. The police confiscated my passport.''

"Your passport? Why?''

"I don't know. I've never even used it. I just kind of keep it around in case, you know?''

"But if you've never used it, why would they even be interested in it?''

Sidney shrugged.

"And where does Albert von Schmidt fit into all of this?''

"I think he wanted me to get fired.''

"You're getting ahead of yourself, Sidney. Who is von Schmidt in relation to Amerigroup?''

"He's a middleman, self-employed. Amerigroup sometimes sells its technological developments overseas. Von Schmidt is what you might call a technology broker. He finds out which foreign company needs what technology and then he finds a sister company in the U.S. that can supply it. That way Amerigroup makes money from the sale, von Schmidt makes money from his commission, and the foreign company gets the technology.''

"How long has von Schmidt been involved with Amerigroup?''

"A little over five years.''

"And nothing untoward happened in all those five years, either with stolen technology or von Schmidt, until you took over as head of research and development?''

"That's right.''

"Then why do you suspect him?"

Sidney looked at Sam and lowered his voice. "I don't have anything concrete. Just a feeling. I know the people I work with. They're my family. None of them would be involved in something like this, and no one would deliberately try to get me into trouble. It has to be an outsider, and von Schmidt is an outsider."

"But in order to gain access to the technology, von Schmidt would have to be working with someone on the inside."

"No," Sidney said quickly. "I already told you that no one would do that to me."

Samantha disagreed, but kept her thoughts to herself. She made a mental note to check out the other employees in Amerigroup's research-and-development department. Particularly the person who'd replaced Sidney. Why would von Schmidt want to get Sidney fired unless it was to put in a new man of his choice? Nothing else made sense.

"So," she said aloud to Sidney, "you think von Schmidt is the key to this whole mess."

"That's right." He shook his head. "It's just too bad you couldn't find some proof of that in his hotel room."

"Well, whatever it is von Schmidt is after, he obviously doesn't have it yet or he wouldn't still be in town."

"I hadn't thought about that."

"You should have told me all of this sooner, Sidney. I feel as though I've wasted a lot of time."

"I'm sorry," he apologized quietly. "But let's face it, you still don't really know what to look for."

Samantha grew quiet. "Did you discuss what you just told me with the head of Amerigroup or anyone else when you were questioned?"

"No. To be honest, I didn't even think of any of this until about a week ago. At first I thought it was just some horrible nightmare of a mix-up. But the more I thought about it, the more convinced I became that what was happening to me was too deliberate to have been a simple mix-up."

"But even after you realized that, you didn't tell anyone?"

Sidney shook his head. "I didn't think it would do any good without proof to go along with it."

"Good."

"Good?"

"The company might have run its own investigation, and then von Schmidt would have been alerted. This way is much better. I just wish you'd told me this in the beginning."

"I'm really sorry, Miss English. I wasn't sure I could trust you."

"What changed your mind?"

Sidney shrugged his narrow shoulders. "I don't know. I guess it's your attitude. You don't treat me like a fool. I think you believe me."

"Of course I believe you. And I want to help. I *will* help. You'll see. You'll be back at Amerigroup before you know it." Then she looked at him curiously. "You *do* want to go back to work there, don't you?"

He nodded and pushed his thick glasses back up on his nose. "I really do. It's the only job I've ever had. It's like my home. The people there are my family. They have to trust me again."

"They will, Sidney. We'll fix everything. Try not to worry too much."

"I'll try, but it's awfully hard." He finished the last of his milk and set the glass on the counter. A perfect little half-moon milk mustache curved over his mouth.

"Oh, Sidney," Samantha said in a motherly tone as she picked up a paper towel and dabbed it off of him.

"What are you planning to do?"

"Several things. I'd like to get inside von Schmidt's hotel room and investigate. You never know what you might find that would be relevant—though I rather doubt that he'd leave anything lying around. And I'd really like to get a look at the bankbooks of some of Amerigroup's other employees to see if there's been any unusual activity," she said, more to herself than to Sidney. "Particularly the new head of research and development. I'd appreciate it if you'd give a list of Amerigroup employee names to Harriet sometime tomorrow. It would be nice if I could examine the personnel files of everyone, but Amerigroup would never just hand them over to me." She grew thoughtful. "Is there any way to get into the offices at Amerigroup?"

Sidney shook his head. "Their building security is almost unbreachable. Besides, you're barking up the wrong tree. I told you . . ."

"I know you did, Sidney, and you're probably right, but we need to look at this case from all angles if we want to get to the truth. And you do want to get to the truth, don't you, Sidney? Even if it's not pleasant."

"I do," he agreed reluctantly.

Samantha looked across the kitchen to the blue digital clock on her microwave. It was five o'clock in the morning, and she hadn't even been to bed yet. "Sidney, I'm really tired."

He pushed his glasses back up on his nose again. "Oh, of course. I'm sorry I stayed so long. I've just been so worried about this. I couldn't sleep." He rose from the chair and started to walk around it, but his foot caught on one of the legs and he pitched forward slightly. Samantha caught him by the arm before he fell all the way to the floor. He looked at her rather sheepishly. "Sorry."

Sidney couldn't have been more than five foot four, an inch shorter than Samantha, and he was painfully thin and awkward. His bow tie was a little crooked, and Samantha straightened it out for him. "Don't worry about anything, Sidney."

He smiled back at her. "I'm glad I called you."

She walked him to the door. "By the way, how did you happen to pick my agency? Did someone recommend me?"

"Not really. I just sort of closed my eyes and called the first number my finger landed on."

"You could have lied, Sidney," she said dryly.

He looked at her blankly for a moment, then smiled. "Oh, yeah. Sorry."

She patted his shoulder and sighed. "That's all right. I suppose someday, somewhere, somehow, someone is going to hire me because they've heard I'm good at my job."

Samantha walked him onto the porch and then stood there and watched as he drove off in his battered VW bug. How anyone could actually believe sweet little Sidney was guilty of stealing anything was beyond her.

She took a deep breath of the early-morning air. The sun was coming up. Traffic was getting a little heavier. She rubbed her eyes and went back into her house, turning off the lights this time as she walked through, and climbed the back stairs to her bedroom. Her clothes fell to the floor in a heap. She left them there and climbed between the cool sheets without even bothering with a nightgown. What an evening.

But as tired as she was, she couldn't sleep. She kept thinking about Pierce Westcott. And the more she tried not to, the clearer his image grew.

With a weary sigh that started at her toes, Samantha turned onto her side and hugged her pillow, unaware that on the other side of town Pierce was standing in front of the living-room bay window of his home, holding a drink and staring unsmilingly into the dawn.

Samantha was up by ten. She didn't have any early appointments, so she put on a pair of faded jeans and a long shirt whose tails came nearly to her knees. She rolled up the sleeves as she went downstairs. Her secretary was at the kitchen counter going through the mail. "Good morning, Harriet," Sam greeted her as she walked across the room to the cupboards.

She didn't raise her dark, frizzily curled hair. "Umm."

Samantha reached for a glass. "Anything interesting?"

Harriet pulled a letter from the small stack and read from it, squinting and pushing her glasses up on her nose. "Well, you've apparently won either a trip for two to Hawaii, a new car, or a cute little headset that plays music while you jog. All you have to do is visit White Hills Resort for the weekend to pick up your prize."

"Gee, I wonder which prize is mine."

Harriet thumbed through some more mail while Samantha watched her. "Why did you call Olivia last night when you couldn't get hold of Mr. White?"

Harriet looked at her in dismay. "Didn't she find someone to get you out of jail?"

"Her grandson. But why did you call her?"

She shook her head. "I'll tell you, Sam, at that hour I didn't know who to call. I tried a few attorneys I just pulled out of the phone book and got either their answering services or no answer at all. And I thought about coming myself but I didn't have the bail money—so I just tried Mrs. W. I've heard her tell you enough times to call her if you ever needed anything—and last night you needed something. With her connections, I knew she'd be able to come up with an attorney to help you, and that whoever she picked would be a *good* lawyer. Better than I'd be able to come up with by searching the phone book." Harriet's slightly protruding teeth worried her lower lip. "I'm really sorry about giving you the wrong room number."

"That's all right. It's my own fault."

Harriet frowned and pushed her glasses up on her nose. "How do you figure that?"

"Oh, not the wrong room number. That *was* your fault. My mistake was breaking into a hotel room at all. There has to be a better way to gather information. A more legitimate way."

The doorbell rang. Harriet started to get up, but Sam waved her back down as she left the kitchen. "I'll get it." When she opened the front door, it was to find Pierce standing there, his shoulder leaning against the door frame. He looked her over thoughtfully, taking in the sleep-mussed hair and clear, makeup-free skin.

"Good morning, Samantha."

Samantha stood there for a moment, not saying anything, but more than a little aware of how glad she was to see him. "Hello, Pierce."

"Did you manage to get some sleep last night?"

"A little. And you?"

"The same." He paused a moment, as though waiting for her to say something. "May I come in?"

"Oh! I'm sorry. Of course." Sam moved away from the door and Pierce walked in, crossing the foyer into the living room. "This is nice," he said, looking around. "Did you redo it yourself?"

"Not the heavy work. Just the painting and some of the wood refinishing. Would you like a cup of coffee?"

"Yes, thank you."

She led him into the kitchen. Harriet looked up from the mail, and her eyes widened as she pushed her glasses up her nose and left her finger there. "Harriet, this is Pierce Westcott, the man who got me out of jail last night."

Harriet extended her hand. "I want a raise," she said in a loud aside to Samantha. Then to Pierce she said, "Are you married?"

"No."

"I *demand* a raise."

"Harriet!" Samantha was one step away from blushing for the first time in years.

"I'm sorry, but if it weren't for my mistake and then my calling Mrs. Westcott, you never would have met him." She gathered her little pile of mail and her cup of coffee as she rose to her full height of nearly six feet, smiling at the two of them, all the while backing out of the kitchen. "I think I'll just go to my office now."

When the door finally swung shut after Harriet, Samantha looked at Pierce and shook her head. "The embarrassment I felt last night pales in comparison to what I'm feeling at this moment."

Samantha watched in fascination as the grooves in Pierce's cheeks deepened. "She's very honest, your Miss Fishbain."

"Appallingly so."

"I see why you can't fire her."

"Then you'd better tell me quickly or she's going to be collecting unemployment compensation." She handed him his coffee and grew more serious. "I realize this isn't a social visit." She gathered her courage. "Am I still a detective?"

"I had a long talk with the man whose room you tried to enter last night, as well as the district attorney."

"And?"

"The charges have been dropped."

Samantha, in a burst of enthusiasm, threw her arms around his neck. "That's wonderful! Thank you." Pierce made no effort to return the hug. It was as though he was made of stone. Samantha, embarrassed yet again, stepped back from him, and her arms dropped to her sides. "Thank you."

"You already said that."

"So I did."

Samantha picked up her coffee mug and held it cradled in both hands.

"Do you break and enter often?" Pierce asked.

"I don't think I want to answer that."

"I'm serious, Samantha. You could get into a lot of trouble—and I'm not necessarily talking about legal problems. What if you had managed to get into the hotel room you wanted and the man had come back and caught you?"

"I'd timed his evening walks. I knew he wouldn't come back for at least another half an hour."

"But what if he had?"

"Then I would have found a way out."

"And what if you couldn't?"

Samantha looked at Pierce curiously. "You sound angry. Why? If or how I could get myself out of a tight situation isn't your concern."

His eyes coolly locked with hers. "My grandmother seems to have grown very fond of you. I'd hate to see you get hurt."

Not exactly a personal declaration, Sam thought. "So would I, believe me. I do what I have to, but I don't take unnecessary chances. Ever. I'm very careful."

"But why break in at all?"

"Because I'm a civilian. I can't get court orders to search anything."

"Then get the district attorney to get a court order for you."

"He can't help me, either. He has to have probable cause. All I can give him is a client who might have some suspicions about what someone else has in his possession or might possibly have in his possession in the future. You're an attorney. You know that's not enough." She searched for the words to make him understand. "I don't steal anything. I don't damage anything. I look. That's all I do. And I don't do it that often. But in this instance, if you could just see my client, you'd understand. He can't prove that someone else is responsible for what's happening to him, but maybe I can."

"There has to be a better way."

"What would you have me do? Walk up to the man and say, 'Excuse me, sir, but are you currently engaged in industrial espionage and would you mind terribly giving me some proof?'"

Pierce's eyes flashed amusement. "You don't think that would work?"

Sam smiled at his unexpectedly droll question. "My intuition tells me no."

Pierce's amusement faded as he continued to gaze at her. Samantha returned the look and wondered what he was thinking. Pierce Westcott was impossible to read.

"Have you ever considered a different line of work?" he finally asked.

"No. I like what I'm doing."

"You keep lousy hours."

"That's the truth."

Pierce looked at his watch. "I have another appointment."

"Of course. I'm sorry I kept you so long."

"You didn't keep me." Brown eyes met blue in a long, silent look. "Goodbye, Samantha. I can find my own way out."

As Samantha watched him leave, a frown furrowed her usually smooth brow. Harriet came back into the kitchen and studied Sam over her shoulder as she poured herself another cup of coffee. "Why didn't you invite him out to lunch?"

"Why would I want to do that?"

"Because he's gorgeous and because I saw the way you looked at him."

"Oh, Harriet, for heaven's sake."

"Don't 'Oh, Harriet,' me. I saw what I saw. And I also noticed the way he looked at you."

"Like an annoying insect he'd like to swat."

Harriet just smiled.

"Why are you looking at me like that?"

Harriet's smile grew larger.

Samantha shook her head. "Harriet, you're going to drive me crazy. Let's just stick to business, all right? What's on the calendar for today?"

Harriet walked to the counter and looked over the daily calendar. "Process serving for the Lawson law firm, a court appearance in the Carstairs case, and then that Poondorken man is coming later this afternoon."

"Oh, about Sidney. He was here last night, so I don't think he'll be keeping his appointment today."

Harriet penciled out Sidney's name. "Okey-dokey."

"Anything else?"

"Nope."

"All right. I have some errands to run, and then I think I'll go shopping."

"Shopping?"

"For a date with Mr. Albert von Schmidt."

"Albert von Schmidt?"

"He's the resident of a certain hotel room. Remember? Mr. 519?"

Harriet's smile held a hint of embarrassment. "I know who he is. I just don't know why you want a date with him."

"Because there has to be a better way to gather information than breaking and entering."

"I still don't understand."

Samantha headed up the stairs to change. "You will, Harriet. You will."

Chapter Three

Samantha, her arms full of clothing boxes, stood outside the same hotel she'd broken into the night before, and waited. She was rewarded after only half an hour by the appearance of her quarry as he strode through the door.

Samantha moved quickly forward and deliberately crashed into him. Boxes spilled everywhere.

"Of all the stupid—" the man began angrily in a German accent, then stopped when he got a good look at the woman he'd run into.

"I'm so sorry," Samantha apologized as she stooped to pick up her things. "I couldn't see where I was walking."

He bent to help her. "That is quite all right. Please allow me to help you."

Sam straightened, her arms full again, and flashed him her most charming smile. "Thank you. My car is only a block away."

The man looked her up and down with appreciative gray eyes as he took the boxes from her. Von Schmidt was better-looking in the light of day than she'd expected. Tall, somewhere in his mid-thirties, with just a wisp of gray in his brown hair.

"I'm Albert von Schmidt," he introduced himself as they walked.

"Samantha English."

"How do you do, Samantha English?"

"I do fine, Mr. von Schmidt." She pointed to her yellow Jeep a few cars away. "There it is."

He carefully placed her boxes in the rear and then turned back to Samantha.

"Thank you," she smiled. "I really appreciate the help."

"Not at all."

Ask me out, she telegraphed to him.

There was an awkward pause. The German looked at his watch. "I'm afraid I have an appointment."

Ask me out, she thought again.

"It was a pleasure meeting you," he said politely. "Perhaps next time you'll consider buying less."

"Perhaps. Perhaps not. I *did* get to meet you." Samantha mentally cringed at her own words.

The man smiled at her, inclined his head and walked away.

"Damn," Samantha swore softly under her breath as she climbed into the Jeep. "I must be slipping."

"Miss English?"

She looked up to find that he'd returned. "I wonder if you'd be my guest at dinner this evening?"

Samantha found it hard to suppress her smile of relief. "I'd like that very much."

"Shall I pick you up—" he looked at his watch again "—around eight o'clock?"

"I'd prefer to meet you at the restaurant, if that's all right."

"Of course. I understand. It's become dangerous in these troubled times for women to accept dates with strangers unless they take certain precautions. I'll see you at Trumps at eight."

"I'll be there."

The German looked her up and down, obviously pleased with what he saw. "Good day."

Samantha watched until he was out of sight, shivering slightly even in the heat. There was something about von Schmidt's eyes...something intangible, but frightening. And she had a dinner date with him when her instincts were telling her to run the other way as fast as she could. "Sidney," she said aloud, "I hope you appreciate this."

When she got to her house, Sidney was once again waiting for her, but this time he was in the kitchen working at a computer while Harriet watched over his shoulder in fascination. Samantha looked over his other shoulder. "What's all this?"

Sidney pressed a few keys before smiling quickly up at her. "You said you wanted to see the personnel files at Amerigroup."

"Yes, but..."

"Everything at Amerigroup is computerized."

Samantha pulled up a chair and watched. "You mean you can get into their files?"

"Just the personnel files."

"Not the research and development files?"

He shook his head. "It's too difficult, even for me."

"How disappointing."

"Here they come," Sidney said triumphantly as the message blinked that he'd gained access. A moment later it asked him whose file he wanted. Sidney stood up and moved aside. "It's all yours, Miss English." He handed her a sheet of paper.

"What's this?"

"The list of Amerigroup employees you asked for. All you have to do is type in the names of the people whose files you want to see."

"That's wonderful. Thank you, Sidney."

"Sure."

"I have some good news myself, Sidney," Sam told him as she sat in front of the computer. "I'm having dinner tonight with Albert von Schmidt."

His eyes widened. "How did you pull that off?"

"Let's just say that I still have it," she said with a smile.

"It?" He looked at her curiously.

Samantha's smile faded. "Never mind, Sidney."

Harriet conspiratorially touched his arm. "I'll explain it to you after the movie."

Samantha studied the list. "What movie?"

"Sidney and I are going to a Bogart film festival at the Fine Arts theater."

Samantha looked from one to the other. Harriet towered over little Sidney by a good eight inches. "You have a date?"

Harriet and Sidney both reached up at the same time to push their glasses back on their respective noses. "Is that all right?" Harriet asked.

Samantha didn't really think it was proper to get involved with clients, but Harriet and Sidney both looked so pleased that she didn't have the heart to say anything. "Of course it's all right."

"What time are you going out?" Harriet asked.

"Eight." Sam looked at her watch. "That gives me six hours to look at these files and take a nap before I have to get dressed."

"A nap?"

"I didn't get much sleep last night, and I probably won't get much tonight. I want to keep an eye on von Schmidt after our date."

"You need a partner," Harriet told her.

"I can't afford a partner. I can barely afford you."

"Well, I guess I can mark that item off of my list of things to do," her secretary sighed.

"Mark what off?"

"Asking for a raise."

"If I weren't so tired I'd laugh." Sam stifled a yawn with her hand. "I better get to this." She typed in the first name and waited for the file. "Have fun, you two."

"Do you want me here in the morning?" Harriet asked.

"Yes. I'll be leaving for the Westcott wedding around ten."

"I'll be here before that."

"All right. Thanks, Harriet."

Samantha spent the next four hours staring at the computer screen, going through the personnel files person by person. When she came to Sidney's file, she paid particular attention. He was obviously considered something of a genius by his former employers.

His work record of fifteen years was immaculate except for the final entry. "Terminated for theft."

She looked down Sidney's list and found the name of the man who had replaced him as head of research and development. Gary Sonders. When she called up his file, the first thing she noticed was how much shorter it was than Sidney's. He hadn't been with the company very long. Only five years. But his record was as clean as Sidney's. There was absolutely nothing there that would implicate him.

Finally she turned the computer off and went upstairs to lie down. She felt as though she had lead weights attached to her legs by the time she got to her bedroom. She pulled the drapes closed until the room was wonderfully cozy, set her alarm clock, slid out of her shoes and stretched out on her stomach across the bed with the most beatific smile curving her mouth. She was sound asleep within seconds.

When her alarm went off at seven o'clock, the only thing Sam moved was her arm as she reached to press the turnoff button. After a few minutes she rolled onto her back and opened her eyes. She stretched her arms high over her head and sighed. Would she ever be able to catch up on her sleep? A few hours here and a few hours there just weren't enough.

Half an hour later she stood in front of a full-length mirror and studied her reflection. The strapless green dress she had on showed off her tan. She'd pulled her red hair away from her face and caught it at the back of her head with a rhinestone-covered banana clip that went from the top of her head to the nape of her neck, allowing her hair to cascade in curls. It was, in effect, an elegant version of a ponytail. As a finishing touch she clipped on rhinestone earrings. Then she stepped back from the mirror, looked at herself and sighed. She really didn't want to do this, but it was the best way to get to know von Schmidt—and maybe even to get into his hotel room without having to resort to breaking in.

With a shake of her head, she picked up her purse and headed downstairs.

It was less than a fifteen-minute drive to the restaurant. She parked about fifty feet from the door. When she entered the lobby she looked around for von Schmidt, but he wasn't there. Then she looked in the bar but he wasn't there either, so she went into the restaurant. The maître d' smiled politely at her. "May I help you?"

"I'm meeting someone here. A Mr. von Schmidt."

He moved behind his desk and looked at the reservations book. "He hasn't arrived yet. Would you like to have a drink in the bar while you wait, or would you prefer that I seat you in the dining room?"

"I'd prefer the dining room."

He inclined his head. "This way, please."

Samantha followed him to a round table with comfortably plush chairs in a quiet corner of the room. She smiled her thanks as she sat in the seat he held out for her. "Would you like something from the bar?"

"Dry sherry, please."

"I'll send someone over with it."

Considering how nervous she was, Samantha managed to look remarkably calm. She even managed to curve her mouth into a hint of a smile. No one watching her could possibly have known what was going on inside of her.

As her eyes roamed the restaurant, they slid over a man a few tables away and then shot back to him. Pierce! What was he doing here?

He had been watching her since her entrance. Now he rose, a drink in his hand, and walked over to her table. "Well, well. We meet again, Sherlock. Eating alone this evening?"

"My date hasn't arrived yet."

"Neither has mine. May I join you for a few minutes?"

"Well, I . . ."

Pierce sat across from her and relaxed back in his chair. At the same time, a waiter brought her dry sherry and quietly left. Pierce raised his glass to her in a silent toast, and Samantha raised hers also, watching him over the rim of her glass.

"You look very serious tonight, Samantha. What are you thinking?"

"That you don't smile very often."

"Does that bother you?"

"I think bother is the wrong word." She searched unsuccessfully for the right one. "I guess I just wonder why."

"Perhaps I'm a man of little humor."

She shook her head. "I know better."

"You don't know me at all."

"Ah, but I've seen your eyes light up." A half smile played at the corners of her mouth as she studied him. "All right. Now it's my turn. What are you thinking?"

Pierce just looked at her. "You're the one with all of the intuition. You tell me."

"All right. I think that, much to your dismay, you've discovered that you like me."

A corner of his mouth lifted. "Intuitive and modest. Why do you think that would dismay me?"

"Because I'm not at all the sort of woman you're used to . . . or the sort you have any use *for*. I'm in a profession I love, and one you loathe. We have absolutely nothing in common except perhaps our family backgrounds, and yet I appeal to you, just as you appeal to me." She sipped her sherry. "How did I do?"

Pierce quietly studied her lovely face. She had put his thoughts into words better than he'd been able to since their first meeting. He'd found himself thinking about her at the oddest times. In the middle of a business conversation; driving his car; even sitting in this restaurant waiting for another woman; when he'd seen her walk in, he'd almost thought she was a figment of his imagination. But she was real. Warm and lovely and very real. And very much to be avoided. She wasn't at all the kind of woman he pictured himself having a future with.

"Pierce?"

He sipped his drink, his eyes on her. "You did well."

"And?"

"And what?"

"Usually when two people are admittedly attracted to each other, they do something about it."

"Not in this instance."

"Why?"

"You know the answer to that as well as I do, Samantha. You and I might as well be from different planets for all that we have in common. Being attracted to a woman was enough when I was young. It's not enough any longer. I want more than that.''

"You're talking about Barbara.''

Pierce didn't say anything.

"You aren't in love with her, you know.''

"Love has nothing to do with it. She's the kind of woman I can live with. Just because you love someone doesn't mean you can live with her.''

Samantha met his gaze with a direct one of her own. "I always thought that loving someone meant not being able to live without them,'' she said softly.

"That's a romantic view, and exactly what I'd expect of you.''

"What's wrong with a romantic view?''

"It's nonsense. You can base an affair on something as tenuous as love, but not a lifetime.''

His words hurt her more than she wanted to admit.

Pierce could see the hurt in her eyes. "Samantha, what's wrong?''

She looked at him quietly. "You're very cynical.''

"Not cynical. Just realistic.''

"Then you undoubtedly don't believe in love at first sight.''

"Undoubtedly. Do you?''

"I didn't used to.''

"What changed your mind?''

"I met you,'' she said softly, realizing as she said it that that was exactly what had happened to her.

"Samantha, there you are!'' A mellow voice drifted to her from about ten feet away.

She looked up to find the German coming toward her. Pierce politely rose. "Albert von Schmidt,'' she said, "I'd like you to meet Pierce Westcott.''

The two men shook hands.

"If you'll excuse me," Pierce said, "I should be getting back to my own table."

The German stopped him as he took the seat next to Samantha. "Please, stay. You'll help us to, as you say in English, break the ice."

Pierce sat down again, but it was with obvious reluctance. "Break the ice?"

Von Schmidt smiled at Samantha. "We only met today when we ran into each other. And I mean that literally. She was in front of my hotel so loaded down with packages she couldn't see and crashed right into me."

Pierce's eyes suddenly narrowed as he trained them on Samantha. "Hotel? What hotel are you staying at?"

Samantha just sat there listening to von Schmidt's answer, outwardly the picture of innocence but inwardly cringing. Pierce knew. And Sam knew that Pierce knew. She'd be hearing about this, no doubt. Another splotch on her already splotchy record.

Pierce's gaze suddenly went past her. Samantha turned her head to see who he was looking at, and there, not surprisingly, was Barbara. When she reached their table, Pierce rose. "Hello, Barbara."

"Hello, darling." She kissed his cheek. Her smile faded as she coolly inclined her blond head toward Sam. "Hello."

"Hi, Barbara. I'd like you to meet Albert von Schmidt," Sam introduced.

The German, who had risen at the same time as Pierce, took Barbara's hand in his and raised it gallantly to his lips. "I hope that the two of you will be able to join us for dinner."

Before Barbara could decline, which Samantha felt sure from her expression she was about to do, Pierce pulled out a chair for her. "We'd be delighted, thank you. Sit down, Barbara."

Barbara did, but frowned at Pierce over her shoulder as he pushed her chair in.

She wasn't the only one who wasn't thrilled. Samantha sent a glare in Pierce's direction that would have blinded him with its intensity if he'd noticed. But he didn't. His attention was focused on Albert von Schmidt. "What line of work are you in, von Schmidt?"

"I'm a salesman of sorts. I'm hired by companies in the U.S. to sell their technology where there's a need for it—at a reasonable market value."

A waiter arrived and took the newcomers' drink orders.

"What Boston-based company are you working with?" Samantha asked.

"Amerigroup. You've probably heard of it."

"I have," Pierce told him. "It's a big company."

"Very. What kind of work are you in, Westcott?"

"I'm an attorney by education but not, for the most part—" he looked in Samantha's direction "—practicing. There are various family businesses I run."

"Westcott," the German said thoughtfully. "Would that be Westcott Publishing?"

"That's one of them, yes."

"Impressive." Albert turned to Samantha and smiled. "You have powerful friends."

Samantha didn't say anything, and he changed the subject. "Did you get your boxes home without further incident?"

"I did, thanks largely to you."

"It was my pleasure. I can't stand to see a woman in distress."

"Lucky for me."

"Particularly such a lovely woman."

The waiter came with the drinks, and Albert von Schmidt raised his glass to the others and made the toast. "To new acquaintances—" he turned to Samantha "—and blossoming friendships."

Barbara looked from Samantha to Albert and couldn't have been more pleased to drink to his toast. The woman obviously felt that if Albert von Schmidt would keep Samantha English away from Pierce that would be perfect.

"I've had a busy day with final wedding preparations," Barbara told Pierce as she set down her glass. "Pierce's sister Jayne is getting married tomorrow," she explained to Albert, "and since I'm her maid of honor, a lot of the planning responsibility has naturally fallen onto my shoulders." Barbara looked as if she'd had a sudden inspiration. "Mr. von Schmidt..."

"Albert, please."

"Albert, then. I can't invite you to the wedding. It's a small, private affair. But I know Jayne would love to have you at the reception as Samantha's escort."

"Oh, I don't know."

Barbara touched his hand. "Please say you'll come. Otherwise poor Samantha will be wandering around all alone."

Albert smiled at Sam. "A sad sight indeed. Of course I'll come. Thank you for the invitation."

Samantha was torn. It would save her from worrying about what he was up to while she was gone. She'd know right where he was at all times. But to have to spend a whole day with him . . .

"And come prepared to spend the night," Barbara added. "There's plenty of room at the beach house to accommodate you. You, too, of course, Samantha."

"Of course." Samantha looked up, straight into Pierce's eyes. He was impossible to read, as always.

Albert lightly touched her arm, sending a shiver of distaste through Samantha. "This will give us a chance to get to know one another better."

Samantha moved her arm slightly away from him. "I'll look forward to it."

"I want to talk to you," Pierce suddenly told Sam as he got to his feet.

"But . . ."

"Now. In the lobby." He took her hand and literally pulled her out of her chair. "Excuse us, please," he apologized to the others at the table. "We'll be right back."

Pierce was so angry he all but dragged her by the arm into the lobby. Samantha finally jerked it away from him and rubbed it. "What do you think you're doing?"

Pierce looked at her in amazement. "*You're* asking *me* what I'm doing? What the hell do you think *you're* doing?"

Samantha pushed her hair behind her ears and waited until she felt calmer before answering. "I'm gathering information for a client," she finally said quietly. "That's my job."

"And is it your job to sleep with a man to get that information?"

She looked at him in amazement. "It's a bit of a leap from dinner to bed, but you seem to have made it easily in your imagination. Your vivid imagination, I might add."

"Samantha..."

"Look," she said softly, "what I choose to do is none of your business, but I'm going to tell you something anyway. I don't like this Albert von Schmidt. I'm not thrilled about having dinner with him, and I'm even less thrilled about having to spend tomorrow in his company. But you said something last night—or was it this morning?—that made sense to me. I don't want to risk getting caught breaking into his hotel room again, so I'm going to try to get in there legitimately. At von Schmidt's invitation."

"Since when do you listen to strangers who give you advice?"

"Since you, the stranger in question, gave me some advice that made sense."

"Samantha—"

"Pierce, this has nothing to do with you. I don't understand what all your concern is about. I've taken care of myself for a long time. Long before you came into my life. And I'll continue to do just that."

Pierce looked at her in silence. He didn't know what he was concerned about either. Until last night he hadn't even known the woman. She was nothing to him. "My concern has to do with the fact that you're a friend of my grandmother's. If you get hurt, she gets hurt and I won't let that happen. What you're doing is wrong. You're getting in over your head.''

"How do you know what's over my head? You don't know me. You don't know anything about me."

"I know that you shouldn't go with him to his hotel room. I don't trust him.''

"First of all, he hasn't invited me to his hotel room yet. Secondly, even if he does and I accept, that doesn't mean that anything is going to happen. I just want to get in there so I can look around.''

"For what?''

"For whatever. I'll know it if I see it.'' Samantha leveled her blue eyes at him. "I don't know why I'm defending myself to you. It's none of your business.''

Pierce dragged his fingers through his hair. "I don't like this.''

"You don't have to like it. It has nothing to do with you.'' Samantha looked at her watch and sighed. "We should be getting back. Your Barbara must be wondering where you disappeared to.''

She started to walk away from him, but Pierce caught her arm. His eyes bored into hers. "Samantha, you be careful with this man.''

"I will. I'm always careful.''

"Even when you're breaking into the wrong hotel room?''

"Will you stop throwing that in my face? It wasn't my fault.''

"I'm not throwing it in your face. I'm making a point. Things can happen—unexpected things—that might have nothing to do with your competence.''

"I understand that.''

He let go of her arm. "Do you have my card with you?"

"It's in my purse."

"Call me if you need me."

"I won't need you, but thank you."

Pierce turned her around and put his hand in the middle of her back to guide her. Samantha suddenly turned around. "Oh, Pierce, there's one little thing."

He waited.

"Von Schmidt is undoubtedly going to ask me what I do for a living."

"So?"

"So I can't very well tell him I'm a private detective. I don't want to do anything that might make him uncomfortable with me. I thought I might tell him that I'm your secretary."

"But Barbara knows better."

"Well, if the subject comes up in front of Barbara, you can distract her while I answer."

Pierce shook his head. "Samantha English, you're trouble. I knew it from the moment I saw you."

"And?"

He cupped her chin in his hand and raised her face to his. "I find myself torn between knowing I should walk away from you and wanting to stay and protect you."

Samantha could feel her heart beating. Her awareness of this man amazed her. Of everything about him. How was it possible?

"Thank you. But I really can take care of myself."

Still they stared at each other. Pierce wasn't even aware that his thumb was stroking her cheek, but Sam was. And it made her tremble.

"We should be getting back," she said quietly.

"I know."

Samantha looked at him a moment longer, then turned and walked back into the dining room. She could feel Pierce behind her. Albert rose at her approach and helped her into her chair. "Barbara and I have been having an interesting conversation."

"About what?" Sam asked as she put her napkin back on her lap.

"About you. She tells me that you're a detective."

Samantha's heart sank, but she didn't miss a beat as she looked across the table at Barbara. "How nice of her to fill you in."

"How long have you been doing that kind of work?"

"Not long."

The waiter returned and took their dinner orders, and afterward, when von Schmidt would have returned to the subject of what Sam did for a living, Pierce ran interference for her, talking about everything from art to politics. Samantha could have kissed him.

Dinner went on and on and on. Samantha didn't think it would ever be over with. Every once in awhile Albert would reach over and touch her hand or her arm. Samantha resisted the urge to recoil. She felt Pierce's eyes on her at times, but she tried not to look at him.

When dinner was finally over, Barbara glanced at her watch and then at Pierce. "I'm sorry to have to leave so abruptly, but I have to drive to Port McKinnon tonight so I can help Jayne get ready for the wedding in the morning."

"I'll take you home." Pierce paid the check and rose, but his eyes were on Samantha. "Good night."

She forced herself to smile up at him. "Good night, Pierce. Barbara."

The German rose and took Barbara's hand in his again and held it for a moment. "It was a pleasure meeting you." Then he shook hands with Pierce. "And you. I'll look forward to seeing both of you tomorrow."

Pierce said nothing, but inclined his head. Samantha could sense his hesitation about leaving her alone with the man, but there wasn't anything she could say to him.

Barbara looped her arm possessively through Pierce's. "Come on, darling."

With one last look at Sam, he left the restaurant. Sam suddenly felt very alone and very vulnerable. She looked at the German and managed a smile.

"Well . . ." He lifted his coffee cup to her. "It's just the two of us."

"Just the two of us."

"You have no idea how much I wish I could invite you back to my hotel."

Samantha knew what was coming next and didn't know whether to be relieved or disappointed. "But?"

"But I have an appointment in just over an hour."

"An appointment? This late at night?"

"In my business one must work at the convenience of others."

"That must be very frustrating for you at times."

"It certainly is. Particularly when I'm in the company of a beautiful woman with whom I'd like to spend more time."

"Thank you, Albert."

He rose and pulled her chair out for her, then put his hand in the middle of her back to guide her out of the restaurant. "The least I can do is walk you to your car."

"You don't have to do that."

"Nonsense. Where did you park?"

She turned to the right. "This way."

It was a nice evening for a walk. Even one this short. Both of them were quiet until they got to the car. Sam took her keys from her purse and then turned and extended her hand to Albert, who surprised her by taking it in both of his and carrying it to his mouth. "I'm looking forward to seeing you tomorrow. Shall we make the drive to Port McKinnon together?"

That was the last thing Sam wanted to do. A plan had begun to formulate during dinner, and she was going to need her own car with her tomorrow to carry it out. "I have to leave quite early if I'm going to be in time for the wedding. I think we should just meet at the reception. Do you know how to get there?"

"Barbara was kind enough to give me directions while you were away from the table."

"That was nice of her. It's really easy to find. I'll see you tomorrow." She retrieved her hand and stepped into the Jeep. "Good night, Albert."

"Good night, Samantha."

As Samantha drove away, she watched his reflection in her rearview mirror. He watched her for a short time, then turned and went back toward the restaurant. Samantha went around the corner and parked, then climbed out and followed him on foot at a distance until he found his own car, a black Mercedes, and climbed behind the wheel. Samantha ducked into a doorway until he passed, then raced back to her car and drove home as quickly as she dared.

Chapter Four

As soon as she got into the house, Sam started stripping. By the time she got to her bedroom she had very little left on, and that fell to the floor within seconds. The evening had grown a little cool, so she pulled a bulky white cableknit sweater over her head. Then she picked up the phone, pressed Harriet's number, and rummaged through a drawer for some jeans as she waited for an answer. It came after two rings.

"Harriet? Hi. It's me. I need to borrow your car." Sam cradled the phone between her ear and shoulder as she hopped first on one foot and then the other in an effort to get the jeans on.

"Borrow my car? Why? What's wrong with yours?"

Sam sat on the edge of her bed and fastened her sneakers. "It's too yellow."

"I could have told you that."

"You *did* tell me that. So, can I borrow it? I'll put in a full tank of gas for you."

"Sure. When do you need it?"

"Now."

"All right."

"Thanks, Harriet. Have the keys ready. I'm on my way."

"What's going on?"

"I don't have time to explain now. Just be ready when I get there."

Samantha hung up and dashed downstairs to her office, where she got out her camera equipment. Then she ran out to her car. If the German was meeting someone later, she was going to be right behind him— unless, of course, the meeting was to be held in his hotel room, in which case there wasn't a thing she could do about it. She only hoped he hadn't already left.

Samantha pulled into the light flow of traffic and sped to Harriet's apartment building. It was only a ten-minute drive, but it seemed like an hour to Samantha. She found a parking spot right in front of the building and pulled into it, stopping with a screech of her tires. She raced into the lobby and pushed the button next to Harriet's name.

"Yes?" came Harriet's voice over the intercom.

"It's me, Harriet."

Harriet pressed a button upstairs that unlocked the door, and Samantha opened it and ran up the steps. Harriet was waiting for her in the doorway, her face smeared with a white facial mask, the keys dangling from her fingertips. Samantha took them and handed

Harriet the keys to her Jeep. "You can drive my car to work in the morning. Where are you parked?"

"Across the street. How did your date go?"

Samantha was already on her way down the hall. "I'll tell you tomorrow," she called over her shoulder.

She found Harriet's car, an old white Ford, just where she'd said it would be, unlocked the door and jumped in. When she turned the key in the ignition, a loud backfire filled the night. The engine took a moment to catch, and even then it was with a slow knocking sound that gradually turned into a fast knocking sound.

Well, she thought, von Schmidt might not see her coming, but he'd certainly hear her.

Samantha was rather surprised when the car actually made it to the hotel. She parked across the street and just sat there staring at the entrance, wondering if there was any way to confirm that he hadn't left yet. At the moment, all she had was a feeling that he was still there. So she waited.

Suddenly someone jerked open the passenger door. Samantha inhaled sharply as a man climbed into the passenger seat. "What are you doing here?"

Pierce closed the door and turned to face her, his arm across the back of the bench seat. "Hello, Samantha. I had a feeling you'd return to the scene of the crime."

"The scene of the—" she began; then paused and said, "Oh." She looked at him in the dim glow of a streetlight. "That still doesn't answer my question. What are you doing here?"

"Making sure you don't get yourself into any more trouble than you're in already."

"I've told you before that I can take care of myself."

"You forget that you're talking to the man who bailed you out of jail."

A smile tugged at her mouth. "I'd like to forget, but you apparently aren't going to let me."

Pierce wasn't amused. "Did you go back to the hotel with him?"

"No. He didn't invite me."

"Would you if he had?"

"Of course. That was one of the reasons I went out with him in the first place. Unfortunately, he said he had a business meeting later tonight."

"It's kind of late for doing business."

"That's what I thought."

"So you're here staking out the hotel."

"If I don't, no one else will. I want to know who he's doing business with."

Pierce studied her in silence for a moment. "Samantha, I think you should get off this case."

"Why?"

"I don't like von Schmidt. I don't like the way he looked at you tonight, and I don't trust him."

Samantha leaned back in the seat and looked at him in surprise. "I thought you were a man who only trusted his intellect, not his instincts."

He ignored that and continued looking at her unsmilingly. "You said something about industrial espionage when we spoke this morning, and if that's what this case is all about, then I think you need to call in someone else."

"Who would you suggest?"

"I don't know. The police. The FBI. Somebody who knows what they're doing."

"It's a nice idea, but I can't call in anyone yet. I don't have enough evidence. I don't have *any* evidence. Just a client's suspicions. They'll take one look at poor Sidney and pigeonhole him as a disgruntled former employee who wants to blame his troubles on someone else. I need something a lot more solid before I can ask for help."

"Are you certain your client's being straight with you, Samantha?"

"Absolutely. If you ever meet Sidney, you'll understand. He couldn't lie if his life depended on it."

"Do *you* understand, Samantha, that if your suspicions are correct, the people involved in this espionage will go to great lengths to protect themselves?"

"I know."

"And von Schmidt knows you're a detective."

"Lots of people are detectives. He has no reason to suspect anything untoward coming from my direction."

Pierce sighed. "I hope you're right, but personally I think you're being naive."

"And I think," she said quietly, "that you're interfering in something that is none of your concern. I appreciate the fact that you're worried about me." A smile touched her mouth. "In fact, I rather like it. I haven't had anyone worried about me for a long time. But it isn't necessary. I'm a big girl and, believe it or not, I can take care of myself. And now," she concluded, "if you don't mind, I have a job to do."

Pierce just sat there.

Samantha looked at him more closely. "I said that I have a job to do."

He lifted an expressive brow as he met her look head-on. "I'm not leaving, if that's what you're hinting at, Samantha, so you might as well just relax."

"But . . ."

"Forget it. I don't want you out here by yourself."

"That's ridiculous."

"Is it? Do you realize that you were sitting on a Boston street after midnight in an unlocked car?"

Samantha could have kicked herself.

"What if I'd been von Schmidt?"

"Then I would have karate-chopped you into submission," she said with a grin.

Pierce shook his head. "Oh, Samantha, what am I going to do with you?"

"Judging from our conversation earlier this evening, you're going to do nothing with me. I'm not your type, remember?" There was no animosity in her tone. Just a cool statement of fact.

Suddenly Samantha spotted an odd-looking little man walking down the street. "Well, I'll be. What timing."

"What are you talking about?"

"Nothing important. I'll be right back." She climbed out of the car and ran across the street after the man.

Pierce watched closely as Samantha and the stranger had a short conversation filled with gestures on both sides. He saw her put some money into the man's hand; then she walked back to the car while the man she'd been talking to retraced his steps and went into a parking garage attached to the hotel.

"Who was that?" Pierce asked as Samantha climbed back in, her eyes on the man.

"Tommy the Toad Simpson."

"Tommy the Toad?" he asked dryly.

"You'd have to see him at a closer range to appreciate how appropriate his nickname is. He's going to find out if von Schmidt's black Mercedes is still in the garage."

Pierce, his mouth twitching, studied her profile. "I can't believe you actually know someone named Tommy the Toad."

"I met him at the jail about a year ago."

"I thought the other night was your first arrest."

"It was. I didn't say I was *in* jail. I said I was *at* the jail, visiting a client. Tommy was there, and we talked. He's a nice man, and he's always full of interesting information."

Pierce rubbed his forehead.

Samantha looked at him and smiled. "What's wrong? Seeing a different side of life?"

"I can't believe I'm involved with a woman who actually knows someone named Tommy the Toad."

Samantha's smile faded. "I wasn't aware that we were involved."

Pierce looked at and then past her. "To know you is to be involved. There's your toad."

Samantha turned in time to see Tommy put his hand to his mouth and cough.

"The signal, no doubt," Pierce remarked.

"The Mercedes is there."

"I feel as though I've walked into a *Barnaby Jones* rerun."

"Wait a minute." Samantha leaned forward over the steering wheel a moment later as the Mercedes slowly pulled out of the parking garage.

"What now?"

"We follow him as inconspicuously as possible." She turned the key in the ignition, and the backfire echoed through the streets like a shotgun blast. "Oh, great. Get down." She ducked her head, and Pierce did as well.

"Smooth," he said dryly.

"Well, maybe if he can't see us he won't know where the noise came from."

"The ball of fire bursting from the tail pipe might give us away, don't you think?"

"You're a lot of fun to have along on a stakeout."

"Where did you get this thing, anyway?"

"It's Harriet's. Isn't it awful? I'm going to have to give her a raise as soon as I can afford to."

"Would you rather take my car? It might be a little less conspicuous."

Samantha smiled at him gratefully. "It's nice of you to offer, thank you."

She peered over the dashboard just in time to see Albert's taillights disappearing around a corner. "We'd better hurry."

Pierce was parked directly behind her. Samantha grabbed her camera equipment and quickly ran to the passenger side of his car while Pierce slid into the driver's seat and started the engine. It idled almost silently for a moment before Pierce put it into gear and pulled out.

They caught up with von Schmidt a few moments later and followed at a reasonable distance. There weren't too many cars on the road, but Pierce used the ones there to his advantage.

"If I didn't know better," Samantha told him admiringly, "I'd say you'd done this before."

Von Schmidt led them to the outskirts of Boston, to a large and very elegant office building with a huge illuminated sign identifying it as Amerigroup.

"I take it this is where your client used to be employed," Pierce guessed.

"Very good."

"And you think von Schmidt is dealing with someone here."

"Right again."

"Do you know who?"

"Not yet. I have my suspicions, though."

"Which are?"

"I think it's the man who replaced Sidney as head of research and development."

"Why?"

"The timing."

Pierce turned off his headlights and parked on the street about two hundred yards from the building, behind some bushes full enough to camouflage the car but not full enough to keep them from watching von Schmidt. Another man—at least it appeared to be a man—was waiting for him in the shadows of the building. They went in together.

Samantha started to open the car door, but Pierce reached across her and held the door closed. "Where do you think you're going?"

"I have to find out who he's meeting."

"How? By breaking into an office building that probably has more security than you ever dreamed of handling?"

"No, of course not." She was intensely aware of his warm arm resting across her lap. "I'm going to get closer to the door and wait there until they come out."

"Did you happen to notice that there are no bushes or trees close to the building? There's no place for you to hide."

"Trust me, they'll never even know I'm there."

He looked past her shoulder and suddenly cupped the back of her head in his hand and drew her toward him. "They won't know you're there because you're going to be here."

"Pierce—"

"Stop talking," he whispered. "We're being watched."

"But—"

Before she could finish whatever feeble protest she started, his mouth captured hers, roughly at first, then becoming gentler. He pulled away slightly and looked into her eyes, a curious frown creasing his forehead. Without saying anything, he lowered his mouth to hers again. And again. He explored the corners of her mouth and moved along her jaw to her earlobe. "There's a policeman coming this way," he whispered warmly against her ear before kissing it and sending a wave of feeling through Samantha. She'd forgotten he'd said they were being watched.

She moved away from him and looked into his eyes as best she could in the dark. "You mean you didn't kiss me because you were overcome with passion?"

"You sound disappointed."

Her mouth was only inches from his. "I am."

Pierce unfastened the clip still in her hair from dinner and watched the red curls fall in thick profusion around her face and shoulders.

There was a sharp knock on the window. Pierce looked over Sam's head. The policeman motioned with his hand, and Pierce lowered the automatic window. "Can we help you, Officer?"

"You can move your car. This isn't lovers' lane, you know." He looked at the two of them more closely. "And you're old enough to know better."

"Sorry, Officer. My wife and I were just making up after a fight. You know how it is."

Samantha smiled at the policeman. Her embarrassment was obvious and sincere. The officer softened. "Yeah, I know how it is. Just don't stay here much longer."

"All right. Thank you." Pierce relaxed against his seat and gazed at Samantha's profile. She, on the other hand, couldn't bring herself to look at him. She watched until the policeman was out of sight, then grabbed her camera and got out of the car before Pierce could stop her. The inside light was on as she leaned back in, her hair falling around either side of her face, and smiled at him, completely without guile. "Bye." She didn't close the door all the way because of the noise. Bent low, she ran across the wide open ground toward the Amerigroup entrance where von Schmidt had gone in, and leaned against the dark building to watch and wait, wondering how on earth she could get in there to see what was going on.

But it was a huge building. Even if she could get inside, she wouldn't know where to go.

She saw a figure coming toward her across the grass and smiled as Pierce came into view. "You just couldn't stay away, eh?"

"Don't push it, Sam. The urge to strangle you rages within me."

Her smile grew broader.

"You are the most incorrigible—"

"Shhhh!"

At that moment von Schmidt, and another man whose face it was impossible to see, come out of the building, talking in low voices. Sam raised her camera with its special night-photography film and took a picture, but she knew it wouldn't do any good. Both men had their backs to the camera, and von Schmidt was even blocking half of the other man's back. The instant the shutter clicked, Pierce jerked the camera out of her hands to keep her from taking another photo. Both men stopped and looked around as though they'd heard something. Sam strained her eyes through the darkness to get a look at the other man, but it was for nothing. All she could see was a vague outline.

After a few moments, the men relaxed and continued their conversation on the way to their cars. Only now did Sam see that there was another black car parked in the darkness. There was no hope of getting a license-plate number. As they climbed into their cars, she heard her camera shutter click and turned to find Pierce taking pictures of the cars as they pulled away from the curb.

Sam wanted to run back to Pierce's car, but he wrapped an arm around her and held her in place until both of the other cars had driven out of sight.

"Are you crazy?" she asked, struggling away from him. "We could have followed them!"

"And they might be waiting for us to do just that, Sam. They might not be certain that someone was here, but they obviously suspect. They heard your camera."

"So what do we do? Just sit here?"

"We'll walk calmly back to my car and then I'll drive you to yours."

"And in the meantime everything I've done today has been for nothing. I don't know any more now than I did when I started this morning."

"Not necessarily. You know that you and your client are on the right track."

"Great."

Pierce took her chin between his fingers and raised her face to his. "You're a hard woman to please."

Samantha forgot all about Sidney Poondorken and his problems for a moment as she gazed into Pierce's dark eyes. "I'm not hard to please," she said softly. "I just know what I want and have a hard time taking no for an answer."

So did Pierce. And as much as he hated to admit it to himself, what he wanted was standing in front of him.

Samantha stepped away from him. "Come on."

The two fell silently into step as they walked across the grass to the car. Pierce held the door for Sam and handed her the camera when she was settled. Then he climbed into the driver's seat and started the engine. Without looking at Samantha, he put the vehicle into gear and drove off.

"Can you give me some more facts of the case, Samantha?"

"You know most of it."

"I want to know all of it."

She studied his profile. "Well, my client's name is Sidney Poondorken."

"Poondorken?"

"That's what I said the first time I met him," she said with a smile. "He was head of research and development at Amerigroup until a few weeks ago, when he was fired from his job and arrested for theft. The company has some proof to back up its accusations."

"Such as?"

"Such as regular and very large deposits into his checking account and a failed lie-detector test."

"And he thinks this von Schmidt is behind things?"

Samantha nodded, her eyes still on his profile. "That's right. And I think von Schmidt's working with the new research and development head."

Pierce was thoughtfully silent for a moment. "Are you sure your client is innocent?"

"Absolutely. He's being framed by someone who knows exactly what he's doing. And the only way to prove Sidney is innocent is to prove that someone else is guilty."

Pierce turned his head, and their eyes met. "I don't know, Samantha," he said quietly. "The more I hear about this, the more I think you've gotten yourself into the middle of something better left to the experts."

"I told you why I can't do that."

"And you're probably right."

They were silent for the rest of the drive. When they got to the hotel, Pierce parked behind Harriet's old car. Samantha sat there for a moment, painfully aware of the man next to her. She was going to have to avoid him if being near him hurt her this much. How strange to think that she'd known him for such a short time. Without saying anything, she started to get out. Pierce stopped her for the second time that night.

"I want your word that you won't go anywhere without telling either Miss Fishbain or me."

"That's ridiculous."

"Promise."

Samantha looked down at his hand on her arm. "I promise."

"And stay away from von Schmidt."

"That's going to be a little difficult considering your Barbara invited him to the reception tomorrow."

"She's not my Barbara, and tomorrow isn't the problem. I'll be able to keep an eye on you tomorrow."

"Oh, for heaven's sake, Pierce..."

He cupped her face in his hands. "If von Schmidt finds out who you are and who you're working for, there's no telling what he might do to protect his own interests."

"I know."

Pierce trailed the back of his hand down her cheek and shook his head. "Of all the women in the world, I have to be attracted to you. Someone who actually knows another human being named Tommy the Toad."

"There's no accounting for tastes."

A smile curved one side of his mouth. "I suppose not. Now go home and get some sleep."

"You, too."

"I'm driving to Port McKinnon tonight. I'll see you at the church tomorrow afternoon."

"All right. Good night, Pierce."

"Night." Pierce waited until she got the other car started, and then they both left.

Neither of them noticed Albert von Schmidt standing at the window of his hotel room, a drink in his hand and a curious frown creasing his forehead as he watched the street below.

Chapter Five

When Sam got home it was past two o'clock in the morning. She slipped into a long silk shirt and climbed into bed, sighing as the sheets settled around her. But as tired as her body was, her mind wouldn't let her sleep. She kept thinking about Sidney's case.

And she kept seeing Pierce's face and remembering the way his mouth felt against hers. Why couldn't he understand that what was between them was more than a physical attraction? It was so clear to her.

She turned onto her side and pummeled her pillow into the right shape before putting her head on it. What if he never understood? What then?

Sam turned onto her other side and pummeled the pillow again. What could she do to make him see? Maybe the best thing to do was nothing.

She rolled onto her back and stared at the ceiling. Doing nothing was the hardest thing of all. She *had* to do something. She could change. She could change into the kind of woman he could live with. Someone comfortable and unchallenging. Never getting into any trouble, completely supportive.

Who was she kidding? She was the woman she was, and if Pierce couldn't accept that, then perhaps she'd be better off without him.

The thought put a knot in her stomach. How could anyone be better off without the person they loved?

Sleep wouldn't come. Samantha went to the kitchen and poured herself a glass of milk, carried it upstairs to her end table, propped up her pillows and settled in for a night of reading. It was a long time later when she finally fell asleep, the light still on, the book still open.

She woke a few hours later without benefit of an alarm, showered, and dressed for the wedding in a feminine, periwinkle-blue linen suit with a full skirt and short jacket, then hoped she wouldn't look as though she'd slept in it by the time she finished the two-hour drive to Port McKinnon.

"Samantha? Are you still here?" Harriet called.

"Just a minute." She threw some things into an overnight bag, grabbed her purse from the dresser and went downstairs. "Hi, Harriet. Still here." She passed her secretary and went into her office to scribble on a notepad. "This is where I'll be in case you need to get in touch with me. I don't know exactly what time I'll get back tomorrow."

"Tomorrow?"

"I'm spending the night in Port McKinnon."

"Ooooooh."

Samantha glanced up from the note. "There's no 'Ooooooh' about it. It's the best way to keep an eye on von Schmidt because he's going to be spending the night in Port McKinnon as well."

Harriet lifted her eyebrows.

"But not with me," Samantha felt compelled to explain. "I mean we'll be in the same house but not in the same room."

Harriet raised her hands. "Hey, what you do with your personal life is your own business."

"That hasn't been true since I hired you."

"Are you telling me that I know about all of your dates?"

"That's right."

"Well, Samantha, if that's the extent of your love life, my heart goes out to you. You've got to get out more."

"I don't have time."

"What you don't have is the inclination. What do you have against dating, anyway?"

Samantha finished the note and handed it to Harriet. "You want the truth? It's too much work. First dates are a nightmare, trying to get to know a man and what he's interested in—besides the obvious. And I'll tell you something, Harriet. There are a lot of shallow men out there. Once you get past the handsome face, there's nothing on the inside to get hold of."

"Who cares?"

"I care. Do you have my car keys?"

Harriet dropped them into Sam's hand.

"Yours are on the hall table along with some gas money. I didn't have time to fill the tank."

"No problem."

She started going through her purse to make sure she had everything. "Do you have any plans for the weekend?"

Harriet got shy suddenly. "I'm having Sidney over for dinner tonight." There was a short pause. "He's adorable, isn't he?"

"Adorable," Sam repeated. "That's a good word for Sidney. Adorable and sweet."

Harriet sighed. "Do you think we look odd together?"

"Odd in what way?"

"You know." Harriet looked at her hopefully. "Well?"

Samantha stopped rummaging through her purse and looked at her secretary. "Truth?"

"Truth."

"All right. I'll admit that when I first saw the two of you together, I was a little taken aback. But I got over it. And I expect that when other people look at you as a couple, some of them will be taken aback as well. But that's not your problem. It's theirs and it's mine. If you two like each other, then nothing should stand in the way of your dating. Certainly not your height and his lack of it. What does that have to do with anything, anyway?"

Harriet smiled at her. "Yeah. Who cares?"

"That's right. It's nobody's business."

"Yeah."

"Yes, not yeah."

"Yes." Harriet looked at her curiously. "Speaking of Sidney, how did your date with von Schmidt go last night?"

Samantha snapped her purse closed and picked up her overnight bag. "Uneventful, for the most part."

"Did you find anything out?"

"Nothing that's very helpful."

"What do you want me to tell Sidney?"

"Tell him that I'll call him as soon as I get back from Port McKinnon." She turned to leave the room, but stopped in the doorway and stood looking around. "I have this feeling I'm forgetting something."

"If you think of it, give me a call. How long do I have to stay today?"

"Until noon. I doubt if anyone will be calling. Just make sure you post the bills. We need the money."

"All right."

"And don't forget to lock up."

"I won't."

Samantha took a deep breath. "I think that's all."

"Then go."

"Right. Oh! I know what I need to take. The Caldwell file. I told Sarah I'd drop it off tomorrow on my way back from Port McKinnon."

"I'll get it." Harriet disappeared, and returned a moment later with the file.

"Thank you. See you tomorrow."

It was a wonderfully warm and sunny day. A perfect day for a drive. A perfect day for a wedding. A perfect day for a reception at a house near the ocean. Weather like this made her glad she had a Jeep. The wind blew her hair into complete disarray, but it felt so good she didn't care.

She turned on the radio for part of the drive, but it grew annoying after a time and she turned it off again. Her thoughts were what she really wanted to turn off, but she couldn't. No matter how she tried to channel her thoughts into a different direction, they always came back to Pierce Westcott. And after this weekend, it would probably be worse.

She moved out of her lane to pass another car, then put on her blinker and moved back. She was driving along the ocean now. The air smelled of salt water. This was the fast way to Port McKinnon. Coming home tomorrow, since she had to stop at the Caldwell house anyway, she thought she'd take the scenic route and take her time. Life was too short to run around at the pace she'd been keeping for the last few months.

The small New England church came into view at that moment. She turned down the tree-lined drive and parked her Jeep next to the row of expensive cars. Samantha climbed out, looked down at her suit and smoothed it with her hands. It didn't look too bad. Then she leaned back into the Jeep and adjusted the rearview mirror so she could see herself. Her hair was a mass of windblown curls. No brush in the world could help her now, so she left it alone. As it was, she was barely going to make it inside before the wedding started.

As she crossed the grass to the church, an usher leaned out of the open white doors and signaled to her to walk faster. Samantha hurried up the steps.

"Which side?" he asked in a whisper.

"Bride's."

He held out his arm and walked her down the aisle to the fourth row from the front, but then Jayne's and Pierce's grandmother saw her and raised her ornate cane to get their attention. The usher looked at Samantha, shrugged his shoulders and walked her to the first row. Olivia, looking every inch the matriarch of a wealthy family, patted the seat next to her. "I thought you were going to miss the ceremony."

"Sorry I'm a little late. I timed the drive wrong," Sam whispered back.

Olivia raised the half glasses that hung suspended by a gold chain around her neck to her eyes and looked Samantha over with a thoroughness which, from anyone else, would have been rude. "You look lovely. But then, you always look lovely."

"So do you." And she did, with her shining white hair waved perfectly in the style of the 1930s, her old-fashioned but still-elegant beige dress with an overlay of lace and several long ropes of pearls.

"Thank you, dear." Olivia dropped her glasses and patted Samantha's hand, then leaned back in the pew with a sigh, staring forlornly at the place where the bride-and-groom-to-be would soon be taking their places.

Samantha looked at her curiously. "What's wrong? Aren't you happy about Jayne's marriage?"

"I'm thrilled. Can't you tell by my smile?"

Sam studied Olivia's profile. "I think a smile is when your mouth curves in the other direction."

"Oh. My mistake." Olivia recomposed her features and pulled her mouth into a tight line. "How's this?"

"I'm overwhelmed."

The older woman relaxed and winked at Sam as her mouth curved into a genuine smile. But then she sighed again as she looked at the altar.

"Olivia, what's wrong?"

"Wimps. They're all wimps."

"Who?"

"The creatures my grandchildren have chosen to marry. Not a stiff spine among them."

Samantha smiled suddenly in understanding.

"Do you find this amusing?" Olivia asked in her best aristocratic voice.

"I find *you* amusing."

The older woman lifted an expressive brow.

"May I be blunt?"

"I'd love to say no, but I have a feeling it wouldn't help."

"I think you'd be disappointed in whomever your grandchildren married."

"Samantha English, you cut me to the quick."

"But it's the truth."

She thought about it for a moment. "Perhaps. But there are exceptions to every rule."

"What's your exception?"

She looked blandly at Samantha. "For instance, I think you're just right for Pierce."

Samantha was startled into silence.

Olivia looked at her in satisfaction. "Took you by surprise, did I?"

"You could say that."

"I thought so the first time we met. I've even tried to get the two of you together, but whenever one of you was available, the other wasn't."

"Is that what all those lunches you invited me to were about?"

"And you never suspected a thing."

"And he never showed up," Samantha reminded her.

"A small detail. It probably wouldn't have done any good anyway. I think he's nearly made up his mind to marry Barbara."

It was a moment before Sam could speak without betraying her feelings. "She's a nice woman."

"Nice? She's perfect. But completely wrong for him."

"How can someone who's perfect be wrong for him? Particularly if that's what he wants?"

"What Pierce really wants and what he thinks he wants are two entirely different things." She looked at Samantha and shook her head. "Men can be so blind at times, unable to see what's right in front of them. You're fresh and interesting and unafraid to feel things."

"That's not entirely true. At least not anymore," she said, more to herself than to Olivia.

"You could teach my grandson to feel things again."

Samantha smiled softly. "Olivia, I think you overestimate my charms."

Olivia's eyes looked into Samantha's. "You and Pierce belong together. I knew it the moment I met you. I think you know it, too. And I hope Pierce figures it out before it's too late."

Sam touched Olivia's hand. "It's starting," she whispered as the soft classical music turned into the bridal march. First the women in the bridal party came down the aisle. Barbara was the maid of honor and looked lovely in her full yellow silk dress. Then came the bride-to-be. But as exquisite as Jayne looked, Samantha found herself looking at the man on whose arm the bride's hand rested. Pierce Westcott.

And almost as though he knew she was looking at him, his eyes went straight to her and remained on her face for several seconds as he slowly made his way down the aisle with his sister.

When they got to the altar, the minister said a few words and then asked who was giving the bride in marriage. Pierce said that he was and then seated himself next to Samantha. He had no choice, because she was where he was supposed to sit.

Samantha looked at him and Pierce looked at her, taking in the mass of stylishly untidy red curls and the clear blue eyes that were deepened today to almost the same color as her suit. Sam offered him a half smile, but Pierce didn't return it. Her heart sank lower as she turned her attention back to the ceremony.

Olivia casually glanced at the two of them, and found herself wishing she were next to her grandson so she could bring her cane down on his foot.

Samantha didn't hear a word. She was too aware of the man next to her. The pew was full, so everyone was closer than they should have been. Pierce's long upper leg rested against Samantha's. She could feel his warmth seep into her through her linen skirt. His arm was pressed to hers, and even sitting there passively she could feel the strength in it.

Sam forced her eyes to remain on the couple in front, but she didn't see them. She was too aware of Pierce's eyes on her profile. All kinds of thoughts raced through her mind, but as the ceremony ended and the bride and groom left the church, Samantha had an almost overwhelming urge to run to her car and drive back to Boston as fast as she could.

But, of course, she couldn't. Albert von Schmidt would be at the reception, and she had to be there too. Someone had to keep an eye on him. And if she didn't spend the night at the Westcotts', chances were good that the German wouldn't either, and that would mess up her plans for later on.

Olivia touched Samantha's arm as they all rose to leave. "I suggest you leave your car here and drive to the house with Pierce. He can arrange to have your car brought over later."

"I really think . . ." Samantha started to protest.

"That's the trouble with today's youth. You think too much. Now do as I say, like a good girl."

Olivia reminded Sam so much of her own grandmother that she had to smile. "Yes, ma'am."

Pierce said nothing, but it was obvious from the way he was looking at his grandmother that he knew exactly what was going on.

Leaning a little more heavily on her cane than usual to generate her grandson's sympathy, Olivia walked away and left Sam and Pierce standing together.

Samantha looked up at him with an apologetic smile. "Sorry about that."

"It's not your fault." He seemed to be looking around for someone.

"Pierce! There you are," Barbara said calmly as she looped her arm through his. "I was wondering why you didn't come out of the church." Then she looked at Samantha and her smile faded a little, as it always seemed to do when she looked at Sam. "I'm driving to the beach house with the other members of the bridal party."

"All right. I'll see you there."

She looked at Pierce and held his arm more closely to her. "The ceremony was lovely, don't you think?"

"It was very nice," he agreed, looking at her closely. Barbara was the picture of perfection. Not a hair out of place. Her makeup was just so on her flawless skin. Barbara was never excited and never depressed. She was always—just right.

Then he looked at Samantha with her tousled hair. She wore makeup, but not much. She didn't need it. There were a few freckles across the bridge of her nose from too much sun, but she'd made no attempt to cover them up. Her eyes were bright with intelligence and humor. A smile was never far off. She looked fresh and wonderful in the linen suit, but then she'd looked wonderful in her old jeans and baggy sweater the night before. And far from being the picture of serenity that Barbara was, Samantha always seemed to be on the edge of some disaster.

Sam had been speaking with another wedding guest, unaware that Pierce was watching her. When she turned back, their eyes locked. What is he thinking? she wondered.

Barbara looked from one to the other and felt a wave of sadness wash over her. In all the time she'd known Pierce Westcott, he'd never once looked at her like that.

Someone bumped into Samantha and broke the spell. She looked at Pierce. "If you don't mind, I think I'd prefer taking my own car. I'll see you at the house."

Pierce reached out and caught Sam's hand as she turned away. "I do mind."

Sam looked down at the hand he held her with and then into his face. "But..."

He moved closer to Samantha but didn't drop her hand. "No buts." Then he turned to the other woman. "We'll see you at the house."

"Barbara, come on!" someone yelled. "They're ready to leave."

Barbara looked at Pierce. Her reluctance to leave Pierce and Samantha alone together was a palpable thing. She reached up and kissed him on the cheek. "See you shortly." And then, with the unruffled sophistication that was so much a part of her, Barbara left the church.

Pierce looked down at Samantha. "Why do I get the feeling that you're trying to run away from me?"

"Perhaps because I am," she answered candidly.

A corner of Pierce's mouth lifted. "I don't bite."

"You don't have to."

Olivia, who was standing at the front of the church, watched the two of them and smiled to herself in satisfaction. Pierce and Samantha might have all the good intentions in the world, but it was going to be to no avail.

Her grandson had met his match at last in Samantha English. Now if he'd only open his eyes and see what was right in front of him...

Chapter Six

Port McKinnon was a small community on the ocean. The residents there, unlike residents of many other small towns in Massachusetts in such picturesque locations, hadn't gone tourist-mad, so there was little traffic and lots of privacy.

The Westcotts' beach house, surrounded by perfectly manicured lawns, was set on a hill overlooking the ocean. As large as the house was, there was about it a kind of Cape Cod warmth and coziness. Cars already crowded the length of the long tree-lined drive, and people were strolling up the drive and around to the ocean side of the house.

Pierce parked in the area reserved for the family and looked at Samantha. "Are you ready to face the hungry mob?"

"The mob is no problem . . ."

"But Albert von Schmidt is another matter entirely," he finished for her.

"He's not a problem, either. I'm almost glad he's coming. At least I won't have to worry about where he is or who he's meeting." She paused for a moment. "When do you think you're going to have my car brought here?"

Pierce looked at her curiously. She'd sounded just a little too innocent. "What's the hurry?"

"There's no hurry. I just wondered. It'll be here tonight, won't it?"

"What if I don't have it brought until tomorrow?"

Samantha took care not to look at him. "That wouldn't be convenient for me."

"Planning on a trip this evening?"

"I don't know. I might want to go for a drive." She looked up at him. "People do sometimes like to go for drives in the evening, you know."

Pierce smiled at her. "You're up to something."

"Don't be ridiculous. You've got a suspicious mind."

"I never used to. Now tell me why you want your car here so badly."

"There's nothing to tell." She started to get out of the car, but Pierce stopped her with a hand on her arm.

"I don't want you doing anything foolish."

"That goes without saying."

"And I don't want you taking off in the middle of the night alone."

Samantha looked from the hand on her arm to Pierce's face. "I don't mean to belabor the point, but what I do in the middle of the night, alone or otherwise, is no one's business but my own. You've got to get rid of the idea that you're responsible for me, Pierce. You're not. And if I recall correctly, you don't want the job."

His grip grew gentler. "I just don't want anything to happen to you."

She studied him quietly. "Pierce, why are you so concerned about me? We're not even friends."

"I don't know." He shook his head, his eyes on hers. "I don't know."

"Well, stop it." She searched for the right words to say what needed to be said. "What I'd really like is for you to just leave me alone. I opened up to you last night and I should never have done that. It's just that what I feel for you took me by surprise. And I took you by surprise. I don't want your pity or your protectiveness. All right?"

"But von Schmidt . . ."

"Albert von Schmidt isn't going to do anything to me. He doesn't even know I'm watching him."

"Famous last words."

"I certainly hope not."

Pierce let go of her arm. "You win, Sherlock. Come on. We have a reception to attend."

They walked up the drive in surprisingly comfortable silence, listening to the chamber music that grew louder the closer they got. The yard was tastefully decorated with lanterns for nightfall, tables laden with artistically displayed food, bright splashes of flowers from gardens that seemed to stretch forever. A seawall separated the ocean, several hundred yards from the house, from the lawn. Some of the guests had already wandered to the seawall to enjoy the view.

"Pierce, there you are," Barbara called as she walked toward them. "I wondered what was holding you up." She looped her arm through his and smiled at him. "Come with me. There are some friends I want you to meet."

Pierce looked at Samantha. Good manners forbade his leaving her alone.

Samantha suddenly spotted Olivia over his shoulder and breathed a sigh of relief. "Excuse me, you two. I think I'll chat with Pierce's grandmother for a while."

Samantha felt Pierce's eyes on her as she walked across the lawn, and wished she could shake the intense awareness she had of the man. Nothing like that had ever happened to her before, and it made her extremely uncomfortable.

Olivia smiled as Samantha approached. "Hello, dear. How are you and my grandson getting along?"

Samantha kissed her cheek. "We aren't, so don't get your hopes up."

Olivia suddenly smiled. Her still remarkably smooth skin crinkled just a little around her eyes. "You're in love with him, aren't you?"

"For all the good it does, yes."

"Then half of my battle is over."

"This is one battle I think you're going to lose. Your grandson has a very clear idea of what he wants in a woman, and I'm afraid I'm not even in the running."

Olivia just smiled. She'd seen the same look that Barbara had seen, and unless she missed her guess, her grandson was beginning to see the light. She put her arm through Samantha's and turned her toward a banquet table, impatiently tapping her cane against the leg of a man in front of them to get him to move out of the way. "Let's have some punch, dear, and then you can mingle with some of the younger people."

"Don't you like my company?"

"I adore your company, but from what I understand from your Miss Fishbain, you don't get out very often. This is a nice chance for you to meet some men and women your own age."

"Miss Fishbain talks too much."

"She's very fond of you."

"That has nothing to do with talking too much."

"I think you're very fond of her, too."

Samantha shook her head. "You're a difficult woman to argue with."

"I know. Most people don't even try."

"I'll take a lesson."

Olivia looked at Samantha and grew more serious. "You're a lovely young woman. Exactly the kind of granddaughter I would have requested if anyone had bothered to ask."

Samantha hugged her. "Thank you."

Olivia hugged her back. "You're welcome. And thank you. Now let's get something to drink."

Waiters circulated among the guests. Olivia imperiously raised her cane, and one came immediately. "You don't really want punch, do you?" she asked Samantha.

"I'd prefer a glass of wine. White."

"Two glasses of white wine," she ordered. "And be quick about it, young man."

As the waiter rushed off, a woman Sam didn't know started a conversation with Olivia. Samantha quietly excused herself and walked toward the bar. The young waiter spotted her and handed her a glass of wine before quickly making his way through the crowd to Olivia.

Samantha took a sip and looked around. There wasn't a single person she knew. Most of the people had broken into small groups and were chatting away. She didn't feel like joining any of them. What she really wanted was to be alone, and she saw the perfect place for exactly that. Taking care not to bump into anyone with her glass, she squeezed through the crowd and headed for the open spaces. No one was at the seawall when she got there. In fact, no one was anywhere near it. Kicking off her shoes, she perched on it facing the ocean and sipped her wine. The breeze washed across her skin and lifted her hair away from her warm neck. This would be a wonderful place to get away to once in awhile.

Pierce, a drink in his hand, leaned his shoulder against a tree fifty feet behind Samantha and watched her. The sunlight caught in her red hair and lent it a lovely glow. Her head was turned slightly, her face raised to the sun, exposing her arched throat and profile to him. The muscle in his jaw grew taut.

At that moment, Samantha, her eyes still closed, turned her head. She slowly opened them right into Pierce's gaze and was still for a moment, as though trying to figure out what he was thinking.

Barbara was speaking with someone else when she glanced in Pierce's direction. When she saw who his eyes were on, her smile grew tight. She walked to where Pierce stood and handed him a small plate of food. "I thought you might be hungry."

Pierce looked down at her and smiled. Sanity returned. He and Barbara shared common values. They had common interests. She wouldn't turn his world upside down the way Samantha would—had.

"Things seem to be going well," Barbara offered as she looked around at the guests.

"I'd say so."

"I did a lot of the planning myself, you know."

"I know. You did a nice job. I'm sure my sister appreciates your efforts."

"What about you?"

He smiled at her. "I appreciate all of your hard work, too."

Pierce took a few bites of food and handed the plate back to Barbara. "You'll have to excuse me, Barbara. I have some business calls to make."

"Oh, Pierce, can't that wait? Surely business can survive one day without you."

His gaze went to Samantha's back. "I'll try not to take too long."

Samantha sat on the seawall for quite awhile, genuinely enjoying herself. She didn't get to the ocean very often. There was nothing quite as restful as the sound of the waves. She could hear them even over the music, which had evolved from chamber to soft rock.

"Hello," said a male voice behind her.

Samantha turned to find Albert von Schmidt standing there. "Hello. Did you have any trouble finding your way?"

"None, though you'd never know that by my tardiness. I hope you haven't been waiting too long."

"Actually, I was enjoying myself. But just out of curiosity, why are you so late?"

He held out his hand to help her down from the wall. "I'm afraid I had a late night and overslept by quite a bit this morning. Of course, you had quite a late night yourself."

Samantha, who'd been putting her shoes on, looked at him quickly. "What do you mean?"

"We didn't leave the restaurant until after midnight."

"Oh," she smiled, "that. I don't live all that far from where we ate."

"So you went straight home, did you?"

"It would have been a little late for a second date," she answered cautiously. "Why do you ask?"

He looked at her for a moment. "No reason. You just strike me as someone with an active social life."

"You're not a very good judge of character, are you, Mr. von Schmidt?"

"Meaning that you *don't* lead an active social life."

"Exactly."

"What a loss to the men of Boston."

"Thank you."

He inclined his head.

Samantha had the strangest feeling that the German knew something. It wasn't anything he'd said. It was just the way he was looking at her. Differently than he had last night. It was eerie.

"So, tell me, Samantha English, how was the wedding this morning?" he asked as they walked toward the main body of guests.

"It was very simple and lovely. You can see for yourself that the bride is exquisite."

He looked toward the middle of the lawn, where Jayne was dancing in the arms of her new husband while everyone else watched. A moment later the others joined them. The German held out his hand. "Come, Samantha. Dance with me."

"Oh, I . . ."

He reached out and took the hand she wouldn't offer and pulled her toward the other dancers, then stopped suddenly and swung her into his arms. She hadn't realized until von Schmidt grabbed her just how strong he was, and that realization did nothing to relax her.

"Loosen up, Samantha. Let your body—your very beautiful body—flow." He pulled her closer to him.

Samantha strained away from him as much as she dared. "I'm afraid I'm not a very good dancer."

"You're a wonderful dancer. You just need to relax a little more."

"I'll try."

"Why are you so tense?"

"Tense? I didn't realize I was."

His hand massaged her back as they danced. "Oh, but you are. I can feel how tight your muscles are."

"Perhaps it's because I haven't danced in awhile. You know how that goes. I'm concentrating on my feet, and that's death when it comes to dancing." She was talking too fast but she couldn't seem to stop.

The hand he was massaging her with moved in a circular motion slowly up and down her back. For the first time in her life, she realized what people meant when they said that someone made their skin crawl. She wanted to jerk herself away from him, but she didn't dare.

A hand came down on the German's shoulder. "Excuse me, but I believe Samantha promised me this dance."

Samantha looked up to find Pierce standing there. She couldn't keep the relief she felt from flooding into her expression. "Oh, Pierce, I forgot. I'm sorry."

Von Schmidt had no choice but to step aside, which he did with a polite bow.

Pierce pulled Samantha lightly into his arms. "You looked terrified. What was he saying to you?"

"Nothing, really."

"You're trembling."

"I don't like him. I don't like it when he touches me."

"Then don't let him touch you."

"That's a little difficult when he's dancing with me."

"Don't dance with him."

"I have to. He's supposed to be my date for the afternoon, remember?"

Though they danced in silence for a time, Samantha could tell that Pierce was angry.

She tilted her head back and looked up at him. "Thank you for rescuing me."

He looked into her blue eyes and softened despite himself. "You're welcome."

Samantha sighed and relaxed. The difference between being held by Albert von Schmidt and being held by Pierce Westcott was amazing. Pierce made her feel warm and safe. This was exactly where she wanted to be. The hand he pressed against her back was firm and didn't roam suggestively the way von Schmidt's had.

Samantha moved almost imperceptibly closer, and then closer still until their bodies were almost, but not quite, touching. Such was their awareness of each other that they didn't have to touch. She turned her head to smile at someone and her hair brushed against Pierce's face. He closed his eyes for a moment at the fragrance. It was fresh and clean, like her.

Another couple bumped into Samantha, pushing her body into Pierce's. He inhaled sharply, but held her where she was. Samantha looked up at him. "It feels right, doesn't it?" she said softly. "It does to me. I think it does to you, too."

"Samantha..."

She placed a finger over his mouth, then rested her cheek on his shoulder. It was growing dark out. The lanterns had been turned on, and their romantic light kept some shadows away but allowed others to come and stay. Sam felt his breath ruffle her hair. It was strangely as though there was no one else around, just the two of them.

Pierce moved his mouth against her hair. Samantha raised her head and looked at him, her face inches from his. "Why are you looking at me like that?" she asked softly.

He pushed her hair away from her face, still swaying to the music. "I'm trying to understand."

Her gaze searched his face. "Understand what?"

"What it is I feel when I'm with you. I want to take you off someplace where we can be alone. Someplace where I can make love to you."

A smile touched her mouth. "What you're feeling is called lust."

They were still swaying gently to the music. Pierce's finger brushed her mouth. "I want to kiss you here." It trailed over her cheek and down her neck. "And here." It moved inside the collar of her blouse and slowly down the V opening, and came to rest at the first fastened button between her breasts. "And here."

Samantha's imagination traveled right along with him. Her breasts rose and fell with her deepening breath. She put her hand over his. "Pierce."

"Ummmm."

"I don't think we should do this."

"Why not?"

"People are watching."

"Let them."

"You don't mean that."

Pierce rested his forehead against hers and turned the hand near her breast over so that he could clasp hers. "You're right."

Samantha sighed.

"What's the matter?"

"I was half hoping I was wrong."

Pierce smiled and moved into a more proper form for dancing, distancing himself from her. "I like your honesty."

"I rather enjoyed your lust."

Pierce laughed. It was a deep, rich sound that delighted her. And then it faded. "It's more than lust."

Samantha looked up at him, studying his strong face. "I know."

"What do you know?"

"That you love me, too. The difference between us, though, is that I accept that I love you. You can't accept that you love me because you don't want to.

Loving me will complicate your life, and you're not a man who likes complications."

"And where does that leave us?"

"Alone," she said softly. "Alone and lonely."

"There'll be other men for you."

Samantha shook her head, a sad little smile playing at the corners of her mouth. "Do you believe in destiny?"

"No."

"I do. You're mine. I knew it when I met you, but I didn't have a word for it. Now I know. And whether you realize it or not, I'm yours. You may marry someone else, but in your heart you'll always be in love with me." Samantha stopped dancing. "Excuse me. I feel like having a drink."

Pierce was filled with an almost indescribable sense of loss as he watched her walk away. But he wouldn't allow himself to follow her. It would pass. It was impossible to fall in love with someone you barely knew.

Wasn't it?

He saw von Schmidt approach Samantha and then walk with her to the bar. He started to go to her then because he didn't trust von Schmidt, but Barbara suddenly planted herself in front of him. "You haven't danced with me once tonight, Pierce."

His eyes still on Samantha, he reluctantly took Barbara into his arms.

"Did you get your work done?" she asked conversationally.

His attention was still elsewhere.

Barbara took his chin in her hand and forced him to look at her. "I asked if you'd gotten your work done."

"Yes."

"Good. Now we can have some fun."

Samantha accepted a glass of wine from von Schmidt. "Thank you." She took a sip as she looked around at the people. "This is lovely, isn't it?"

Von Schmidt eyed her smooth profile. "Yes, quite."

Samantha took another sip and looked at him over the rim of her glass.

"What would you say to the two of us taking a quiet walk along the ocean?" he asked.

"I'd say a polite 'No, thank you.'"

"I know how to be a gentleman."

She smiled, not at all won over. "I'm sure you do, but the answer is still no. I'm a little tired. I really don't feel like taking a walk."

"Your late night is catching up with you."

Sam looked at him curiously. That was the second time he'd made a reference to her late night. Had he somehow spotted her following him last night? But she dismissed the thought almost as soon as it came into her mind. It was impossible. He couldn't have. They'd been too careful.

She looked across the dwindling sea of people and saw Pierce dancing with Barbara. Barbara was doing all of the talking. Pierce's mind seemed to be elsewhere.

She took another sip of wine and sighed.

"I realize I'm not the most exhilarating companion in the world, but I'm not that bad."

Sam smiled apologetically at von Schmidt. "I'm really sorry. I've all but yawned in your face."

"That would have been a real ego boost," he said dryly.

"Most of the guests seem to be leaving. I think I'll just go up to my room now and try to get some sleep."

"I'll walk you in."

"There's no need. You stay and enjoy the music. There must be a dozen lovely women left for you to dance with."

"Are you sure you don't mind?"

"I insist. Otherwise I'll be feeling guilty and I'll never get to sleep. You wouldn't want that on your conscience, would you?"

"Not if I can avoid it."

"Then stay and have fun. I'll see you in the morning."

Von Schmidt kissed her cheek, and Samantha made herself stand still for it. "Good night," he said softly. "Sweet dreams."

"They're the only kind to have. Good night."

Samantha walked across the lawn and into the house, hoping that somewhere along the way she'd bump into someone who could tell her where to go.

"Samantha?"

She turned, her hand over her heart, and found Pierce's tall figure filling the doorway behind her. "You shouldn't sneak up on a person like that."

"I didn't sneak. I live here, remember?"

"I remember."

"What are you doing?"

"I'm trying to find out which room I have for the night."

"Going to bed already?"

"I'd hardly say 'already.' It's after midnight."

"That's early."

"For you, perhaps. For me, it's late and I'm tired. I haven't been sleeping well lately."

He studied her quietly. "Open your windows tonight, then. The sound of the ocean is sort of a natural tranquilizer. Maybe that will help you sleep."

Samantha didn't say anything. She had a long night ahead of her, and it didn't include a lot of sleep.

"You *are* going to sleep, aren't you?" he asked as he moved farther into the room.

She couldn't look him in the eye. "I'm certainly going to try." Samantha hesitated. "By the way, could you tell me if my car was brought here from the church yet?"

"Why?"

"My suitcase was in it."

"It got here a few hours ago. Your suitcase has already been taken to your room."

"Thank you. And do you happen to know which room is mine?"

"No, but I know who to ask."

"Then would you please?"

Pierce watched her for a few more seconds, then turned and left the house. A woman entered a minute later and smiled pleasantly. "Mr. Westcott asked me to show you to your room."

"Thank you."

"Not at all. Follow me, please."

Samantha did. The woman took her to a lovely room that overlooked the ocean and the party. Sam left the room in darkness as she closed the door behind the woman and walked to the window to look out. She saw Albert von Schmidt dancing and enjoying himself. Barbara was in a circle of people, drinking champagne and talking. Even Olivia was still there, seated comfortably as though holding court, watching her guests enjoying themselves.

Samantha spotted her suitcase in the moonlight streaming in through the window and smiled her silent thanks to the Westcotts and their efficient household. She quickly rummaged through the contents until she found her jeans and a dark blue sweater. It only took her a minute to change. Then she brushed her hair into a careless ponytail. The only problem would come if whoever had brought her car hadn't left the keys in it. She hadn't dared to ask Pierce where they were. He was suspicious enough without her adding to it.

With another quick look out the window to confirm where von Schmidt was, she left the room and made her way carefully through the house and out the front door. No one was there at all. Everyone was on the ocean side.

She spotted her car, which showed up in the dark even at a distance, and ran quickly across the lawn. When she got there she reached inside, mentally crossing her fingers, and smiled when she found her keys safely in the ignition.

Glancing around to see if anyone was watching and finding no one, Sam climbed into the Jeep and started the engine, grimacing at the noise, slight though it was. With exquisite care, she backed out of the parking space and then sort of let the Jeep roll forward on its own, without pressing the accelerator, until she was out of earshot of the house.

Another car engine started as soon as hers was out of sight. Pierce, his headlights off, waited several seconds before following her down the drive and onto the main road. What was she up to this time? he wondered.

Chapter Seven

As soon as he realized she was headed back to Boston, Pierce thought he knew where she was going, but he kept his distance anyway, not quite sure and unwilling to take the chance of losing her.

The traffic was light when they got into Boston. It got a little more difficult for Pierce to stay out of sight. Samantha went through a green light that turned yellow just as she passed. Pierce didn't want her to get that far ahead, so he went faster, but didn't quite make it before it turned red. There were no cars coming, so he ran it. A moment later the lights of a police car flashed behind him. Swearing softly under his breath, Pierce pulled to the side of the road and got out his wallet.

Samantha found a parking place right in front of the hotel. She glanced cautiously up and down the street and discovered she was quite alone.

For the second time in a few days, she walked into the hotel lobby as though she had a perfect right to be there and took the elevator to the fifth floor. This time she found the right room, and a click from her lock pick told her a few minutes later that she was home free. She could search to her heart's content because von Schmidt was nowhere near Boston, thanks to Barbara Lowell.

Von Schmidt had a suite. Sam went through the living area first, flashlight in hand, checking under couch cushions, the linings of the draperies, the refrigerator and all through the bar. Nothing was there except what should have been. Then she went into the bedroom and methodically started her search all over again, checking every item of clothing, every towel, every curtain, and putting everything back exactly the way von Schmidt had left it.

A message light on the telephone blinked red. Samantha only thought about it for a moment before shining the beam of the flashlight onto the dial and calling the hotel operator. "Hello. I believe you have a message for room 591."

There was a brief pause while the woman found the appropriate note. "Yes. But it's for Mr. von Schmidt."

"That's all right. I'm Mrs. von Schmidt."

"Very well. It says that the meeting is on for Monday at eleven o'clock p.m., usual place."

Samantha waited for her to finish the message but, when there was silence, asked the obvious question. "Who placed the call?"

"There was no name. He said Mr. von Schmidt would know who it was."

"I see. Thank you very much."

Sam hung up the phone and was getting ready to leave when she heard a key slide into the sitting-room door. She raced into the bedroom and shone her flashlight around quickly, looking for a place to hide and not finding any. Who could it be, anyway?

The door opened. Samantha turned off her flashlight and moved quietly across the bedroom to the window, which she slid open with exquisite care, thanking the powers that be that this wasn't one of those modern hotels where everything was sealed, and slipped outside to the foot-wide ledge.

Samantha's heart was in her throat as she slowly turned to face the building and clung to the cement overhang above the window. A fine film of perspiration broke out all over her body as she told herself over and over again not to look down. But even with her eyes closed she could visualize the ground clearly. It was silly to be afraid of heights. Samantha knew it. She was perfectly secure on the ledge. It was nice and wide.

She took a deep breath and held it. Then another and another. Slowly, forcing herself to concentrate on her breathing so she wouldn't hyperventilate.

A light flashed on in the bedroom. Samantha opened one eye and then the other and peered in through the half-open blinds. It was von Schmidt. What was he doing here? He was supposed to be sleeping peacefully in Port McKinnon by now. Von Schmidt stood in the doorway and looked around the room. It was a strange look. Almost as though he expected something to be out of place. Did he suspect something? And if he did, why?

He walked over to the phone and dialed a single number. That meant he was calling someone in the hotel. "Operator," she heard him say through the open window, "do you have any messages for room 591?"

There was a pause. "Mrs. von Schmidt picked it up?"

"Damn," Samantha whispered under breath.

"How long ago? I see. Thank you."

He was sitting on the edge of the bed staring at the window. Staring right at her, but not seeing her.

He suddenly walked toward the window and Samantha froze, sure he'd seen her. His face was only inches from hers as he slid the window shut, but he hadn't seen her. Samantha took a deep breath and slowly exhaled. Bless the darkness.

A moment later the light went out in the bedroom and then in the living room. She felt rather than heard him close the door to the room. Sam stayed there a little longer just to make sure he was gone before trying to open the window. It was locked! She set the flashlight down on the ledge to free her hand and pulled on the window as hard as she dared, but it wouldn't budge.

Her foot accidentally nudged the flashlight, and it fell off the ledge onto the street below. She looked down as it fell, but had to look away and catch herself on the cement overhang as a wave of faintness engulfed her.

The flashlight shattered on the pavement a few feet in front of Pierce as he walked along the side of the hotel. He looked up, and his heart went into his throat.

"Samantha, what in the hell are you doing?" he called up.

Sam had never been so happy to hear a voice in her life. "Pierce! Help me, please."

"Of all the reckless, stupid . . ."

Samantha took several deep breaths, determined to control her fear, and looked down at him. Her knees started to buckle, and she had to press her face against the window.

Pierce saw her sway and instantly knew what was wrong. "Samantha, I'm coming up the fire escape." His calm voice belied the terror that filled him. If anything happened to her... "Just hold on, Sam." He talked as he climbed. "Pretend you're standing on the ground. You have all the room in the world. There's nothing to be afraid of."

Samantha concentrated on the noise Pierce's shoes made on the metal fire escape that zigzagged its way down the side of the building.

"I'm level with you now, Samantha," Pierce said softly. "I'm going to make my way along the ledge to you." Even as he spoke he inched his way carefully along. A moment later he was there, and he wrapped one arm around her waist as he held on to the cement overhang with the other hand. "Come on. We'll go back together."

Samantha's breath came in short bursts. "I can't. I want to, but I can't move."

"Of course you can. Do what I told you to a few minutes ago. Imagine you're on the ground. Someone has painted a line you don't want to cross, so you have to make your way past it carefully. I'll guide you.

There's no reason for you to look down. Can you do that for me, Samantha?"

"I'll try. God, I hate being afraid like this. And I'm sorry you got dragged into it."

"Apologize after we're on the fire escape."

"I just wanted to make sure it got said in case we don't make it."

"I love an optimistic woman. Come on, Sam." His grip tightened comfortingly around her waist. "Let's start."

Side step by slow side step they made their way along. The sound of Samantha's heartbeat throbbed in her ears. She stopped about halfway to the fire escape and leaned her forehead against the bricks. Pierce moved his body closer to hers. "You're doing fine," he said softly. "We don't have much further."

Samantha swallowed hard and licked her dry lips.

"Ready?"

She nodded.

"All right. Here we go again. Just a few more steps. You can do it," he patiently coaxed.

It seemed like forever, but in reality it had taken Pierce less than ten minutes to get her to the fire escape. He stepped onto it first, then put his hands at Sam's waist and lifted her onto it.

"You're safe now."

Samantha dug her fingers into his shoulders and buried her face in his chest. Her entire body quaked. Pierce gathered her into his arms and held her as tightly as he could, not sure how much of the quaking was hers and how much was his. He kissed the top of her head, stroking her hair. "It's all right," he said over and over again.

Suddenly she moved away from him. "No, it's not all right. I could have gotten you killed." Tears streamed down her face.

"But you didn't. We're both fine."

"You're fine. I should be shut up someplace where I can't do crazy things anymore."

"I think you're being a little hard on yourself, Samantha. That's *my* job."

"Then do your job and let me have it."

"I will. Believe me, I will. But not right now."

"Why not?"

"Because right now all I can think about is how glad I am that you're safe. If anything had happened to you . . ." He shook his head, unable to finish the sentence.

Samantha sniffed. "If anything had happened to me what?"

Pierce cupped her face in his hands and wiped away her tears with his thumbs. "I would have been a most miserable man."

"You would have been well rid of me."

"Probably." His mouth curved at her offended look. "Let's get our feet on the ground."

Samantha followed him down the five flights of fire escape stairs, again not looking down, but with her eyes glued to his back.

When they were on the ground, he wordlessly walked her to a coffee shop across the street and ordered a cup for both of them. Samantha looked at him across the table. "What are you doing in Boston?"

"Rescuing damsels in distress."

"You know what I mean."

He smiled at her. "Yes, I know what you mean. I had a feeling you were up to something when you decided to go to bed early, so I waited in my car, and sure enough, a few minutes later there you were, sneaking down the drive."

"I wasn't sneaking. I was being cautiously quiet."

"You were sneaking."

"All right, all right. If you insist."

"Oh, I do."

"And what do you call what you were doing?"

"Following a sneak."

Samantha's dimple flashed. "I like that."

"I thought you might."

"And I'm glad you did. I'd still be up there on that window ledge if you hadn't."

Pierce tapped her cup. "Drink some. How did you get out on that ledge anyway?"

Samantha cradled the cup in her hands, savoring its warmth. She still felt chilled. Fear had a way of doing that. "Everything was fine at first. I got into the room all right. I'd searched the living room and was just finishing up the bedroom when I heard a key in the lock."

"Von Schmidt?"

"That's right. I couldn't believe it. And there was nowhere to hide, so I went out the window. I was so afraid von Schmidt would find me that I forgot my fear of heights. Anyway, he looked around the suite as though expecting to find someone there, and when he didn't, he closed the window and left."

"And there you were."

"And there I was," she agreed, studying him. "You're being awfully nice about all of this."

"We're in a public place."

She smiled again.

"You said that von Schmidt seemed to be expecting to find someone in his hotel room. Do you think he knows you were there?"

"He knows someone was."

"How?"

"Because while I was out on the ledge I heard him call the hotel operator and ask for his messages. I'd already done that and told her I was Mrs. von Schmidt. She apparently told him that Mrs. von Schmidt had just called."

Pierce looked at her and sighed. "So he does know."

"He knows something. Not necessarily that it was me."

"I want you off this case, Samantha. As of this moment. I don't care how worthy your Mr. Poondorken is."

"I can't desert him."

Pierce took her hand in his and gripped it tightly. "I won't have you putting yourself at risk any more than you already have, Samantha."

She pulled her hand out of his and leaned back in her chair. "You don't tell me what to do, Pierce Westcott."

"Someone obviously has to."

"There's no need to be insulting."

"What I'm being is realistic. How long do you think you can get away with this before von Schmidt catches you?"

"As long as it takes."

Pierce dragged his fingers through his hair. "You are the most frustrating woman I've ever met."

"I accept all superlatives." Sam sighed. "I can't quit this case, Pierce. Sidney's counting on me, and there isn't anyone else to help him. Besides, I'm onto something."

"Onto something," he said in disgust. "What are you onto besides trouble?"

"You know that telephone message I mentioned?"

"What about it?"

"It was from von Schmidt's contact inside Amerigroup—I think. A meeting is scheduled for tomorrow night at eleven."

"But he now knows that someone picked up that message. If the man has any brains at all, he'll change his plans."

"I hadn't thought about that." Samantha sighed, deflated.

"Then think about it now. You're flogging a dead horse."

"Maybe. And maybe not."

Pierce leaned back in his chair and looked around the empty coffee shop for a moment before his eyes came back to her. "Samantha, what am I going to do with you?"

"You could accept me as I am," she suggested.

"A novel approach."

"For you, apparently."

Pierce looked at his watch. "We should be starting back for Port McKinnon."

"What time is it?"

"Nearly three. We can go back in my car. I'll drive you here tomorrow to pick up yours."

"No, thank you. I'm going to need mine tomorrow. I'd rather be independent."

"Samantha..."

"Von Schmidt is going to be wondering where my car is in the morning if it's suddenly not there."

He had to admit she was right. "Then you follow me back. No detours, all right?"

"All right."

He shook his head. "Why do I have this feeling that I should keep my eyes glued to my rearview mirror all the way back home?"

"I wouldn't know, but I can assure you it's not necessary."

He tossed some money on the table and rose. "Come on, Sherlock. Let's go."

When they got back to Port McKinnon two hours later, the first thing Sam noticed was that von Schmidt's car was missing. He hadn't gotten back yet. She parked in the same place she'd been before and climbed out. Pierce parked next to her. The house and grounds were shrouded in the darkness that came just before dawn. All of the partygoers had gone home.

Pierce placed his hand in the middle of Sam's back as they walked toward the house. "I wonder where von Schmidt is?" Sam wondered aloud. "He left the hotel long before I did."

"Maybe he's not coming back."

"Or maybe he had some errands to run."

"At this time of night?"

"I didn't say they were legitimate."

Pierce opened the door for Sam and followed her inside. "You go upstairs and get some sleep."

Sam, her foot on the bottom step, turned and looked at him. "What about you?"

"I think I'm going to stay down here for a few minutes and have a drink."

"Then I will, too. I don't think I could sleep right now anyway."

"Tell me, how long has it been since you spent the entire night in a bed?"

Samantha's quick smile flashed. "Is that an invitation?"

A corner of his mouth lifted as he held out his hand to her. "Come on."

They went into the library. He poured two cognacs and handed one to her, then flipped a switch on a speaker on his desk. "What's that?" Samantha asked.

"It's attached to outdoor microphones as part of the security system. We'll be able to hear von Schmidt drive up." Pierce turned out the lights and sat on the couch next to Samantha. There was no moonlight at this hour, so it was quite dark.

Samantha sipped the cognac and sighed. There was something very peaceful about sitting quietly in the dark with someone you trusted and loved—even if it was at opposite ends of the couch.

"Samantha?"

"Umm?"

"Who are you?"

She smiled into the darkness. "That's a challenging question to answer."

"You seem to be so many different people, all wrapped up in one compact body. One minute you're breaking and entering; the next you're dangling five stories over my head and the next you're sitting here quietly, your presence bringing me a peace I've never known with anyone else."

"You'd better watch it, Pierce. You might just fall in love with me yet."

"Do you always say what you think?"

"Most of the time. Not always." She set her cognac on the table next to the couch and stretched out, resting her head on Pierce's lap and closing her eyes. "I'm so tired."

Pierce was taken aback at first. He looked down at her and could see her vaguely now that his eyes had adjusted to the dark. With his free hand he began lightly stroking her hair away from her face.

Samantha sighed. "That feels nice."

"I'd have to agree."

She smiled and rolled onto her back so she could look up at him. They were very still for a moment; then she raised her hand and trailed her fingers over his beard-stubbled cheek. "You need to shave."

"I wasn't expecting to be in a lady's company at this hour." He caught her hand in his and brought her soft palm to his mouth.

"You strike me as a man who's always prepared."

"Except where you're concerned."

"Just think how boring the past few days would have been without me."

"You don't actually expect me to admit to something like that, do you, Sam?" He returned her hand to her.

"Not really," she said softly. "You're a man who rarely lets his guard down. You'd rather be safe than sorry."

"I don't apologize for that."

"I wasn't asking for an apology, Pierce. I'm just trying to understand how you can feel about me the way I think you do and still hold back."

"It's what's best for both of us. There isn't a way in the world we could ever live together."

"But what about this—thing—between us?"

Pierce gazed unsmilingly down at her. "That's what's so nice about being an adult. Just because it's there doesn't mean we have to act on it."

Samantha lowered her eyes to hide the hurt. She hadn't gone looking for love. It had just happened. Happened so quickly and unexpectedly that there wasn't anything she could have done that would have prevented it. She was meant to be with this man. But Pierce didn't want her. He wouldn't let himself want her.

"Listen," he said suddenly.

Sam did. There was a noise on the speaker that grew louder. It was clearly a car engine. It stopped, and a moment later a car door opened and closed. Then there was silence.

"What's going on?" she asked in a whisper.

"I don't know." He paused and listened again. "We should have heard his footsteps by now."

Samantha sat up as if that would help her to hear better. Almost five silent minutes went by. Then they again heard a car door open and close. This time footsteps approached the house. Samantha tiptoed to the library door and cracked it open so she could see the darkened foyer. Von Schmidt slowly opened the front door and just as carefully closed it. He held a handkerchief and wiped his hands on it as he quietly made his way up the stairs and to his room. Sam closed the door and turned to Pierce, a curious frown creasing her forehead. "I wonder what he was doing all that time?"

Pierce had turned on a small desk lamp and was silently pouring himself another cognac.

"Do you think he knows we were in Boston?" she asked.

"I'd say he probably suspects you were. Your car is a little conspicuous, and it was parked right in front of the hotel."

"That was a mistake."

"No kidding."

"I just never imagined he'd show up in Boston tonight. He was having such a good time here."

Suddenly Pierce walked over to her, cupped her face in his hands and raised her eyes to his. "I don't suppose there's anything I can say to you to make you drop this case, is there?"

"I'm not a quitter."

His eyes searched hers. "I have a bad feeling about this man, Samantha."

"So do I. That's why I went out the window rather than braving confrontation in his room."

"You're so stubborn."

"No, I'm not." She looked deeply into his eyes. "To me, stubbornness is when you won't back down even when you know you're wrong. I'm not that way. I'm tenacious. I stick with a project until it's completed. Von Schmidt is guilty of stealing American technology and selling to the highest bidder, and more than that, he's guilty of deliberately setting up a poor little man to lose his job and to spend time in prison. I'm the only defense Sidney has, and I'm not going to toss him over just when I'm getting close to the proof he needs. You wouldn't either if you were in my place."

Pierce's hands fell to his side. "Probably not." He walked across the library and got his cognac, then switched off the light and stood staring out the window with his back to her. "Good night, Samantha."

She stared at his back for a moment, then slowly turned and left the room.

When Pierce heard her leave, he tossed the cognac back in one swallow. Damn Samantha English. His life had been so settled before she'd come into it. She was complicating everything, and she had no right to. No right at all.

When Samantha got to her room, she closed the door and leaned her back against it. She felt empty inside. Hollow. She was going to have to face the fact that in the matter of strong will, she'd met her match in Pierce Westcott. If only she could go back in time to when she'd been arrested at the hotel and change things. She might never even have met him. None of this would have happened.

But she couldn't.

Chapter Eight

Samantha got up just a few hours after going to bed, showered and dressed in her jeans and an oversized shirt that she belted in at the waist. When she got downstairs she found Pierce already there. He'd obviously showered as well because his hair was still wet. His eyes came to rest on her suitcase. "Leaving already?"

"I thought you'd be pleased."

"There's no need to run away. You could at least stay for breakfast."

"I never run away, and I would stay for breakfast if I were hungry—which I'm not." She straightened the strap of her shoulder bag. "I'd appreciate it if you'd thank Olivia for having me here. Tell her I'll call her later in the week."

"If you stayed you could tell her yourself."

"I'm aware of that."

"And what about von Schmidt?"

"I went past his door a few minutes ago. He's still sleeping. Since we're not driving back together there's no sense in my waiting for him."

"You seem to be having trouble looking at me this morning, Samantha."

She raised her gaze to his. He had the most wonderful brown eyes. So dark and unexpected. So easy to become lost in. "How's that?"

"Better. What's wrong with you this morning?"

"Nothing's wrong. I just did some thinking last night and made a few decisions."

"What kind of decisions?"

"Ones I think you'll like. The last thing I want is to be a thorn in your side. You know how I feel about you and I know how you feel about me, and I'm giving up."

"Samantha English, giving up?"

"You said something last night that got me thinking. You said I was stubborn and I denied it. I defined stubbornness as not backing down even when you know you're wrong." Her eyes lingered on his face. "I was wrong. I feel so strongly about you that I thought I could make you feel the same way about me. I felt connected to you the first time we met, and that feeling has gotten stronger. I couldn't imagine that you didn't feel that same connection, but you've finally convinced me. I guess I've made something of a fool out of myself."

"You could never make a fool of yourself."

Samantha's dimple flashed and then faded. "Thank you for that at least. Anyway, as I said, I won't be bothering you anymore."

"Samantha, I do care about you."

"That's kind of you, but it's not enough for me." She walked past him, but stopped and turned back. "You're making a mistake in letting me go, you know. Goodbye, Pierce."

When she got outside, Samantha stopped for a moment and took a deep breath. There. She'd done it. It was over. Finished. For Pierce, at least.

Pierce stood silently staring at the door long after it had closed behind Sam, unaware that his grandmother was watching him from the top of the stairs. "Good morning, dear."

He looked at her unsmilingly as she made her way down the stairs. "Grandmother."

"Was that Samantha who just left?"

He looked at the door again. "Yes."

"I was hoping she'd stay for breakfast."

Pierce didn't say anything.

"Are you staying?" she asked, making it obvious from her tone that she wanted him to.

Pierce took a deep breath and tried to push Samantha out of his mind. "Of course." He helped her down the few remaining steps and walked with her into the dining room, where places had already been set.

"We haven't had a chance to talk for a long time." Olivia smiled at him over her shoulder as he helped her into a chair and then took one across from her.

"Is something on your mind?" he asked.

"You could say that."

"Anything I can help you with?"

"It isn't a matter of helping me, dear. It's a matter of helping yourself."

Pierce looked at her in silence, knowing full well what was coming.

"You and Samantha belong together. Hasn't it occurred to you that there must be a reason why you've known Barbara Lowell for all these years and haven't bothered to propose? It's because even though she's exactly the kind of woman you know you *should* marry, she isn't the woman to whom you *want* to be married."

"Grandmother, please. I've had enough for one morning."

"Apparently not. I've seen changes in you lately that have given me more pleasure than you could imagine."

"Such as?"

"You've always prided yourself on your cold logic and your lack of emotion. But since Samantha came into your life you've begun to feel things. You've begun to see things through her delightful eyes. You've begun to understand what loving someone feels like." Olivia studied her grandson. "One can't choose with whom one will fall in love. It just happens."

Pierce said nothing.

"Samantha is perfect for you."

"Grandmother, you know as well as I do that if ever there were two completely different people in the world, Samantha English and I are the ones."

"And you complement each other beautifully. Where she's carried away by her emotions, you can use your logic. Where you get carried away by your logic, she can share her emotions."

"You forget what a responsibility being married to a Westcott is."

"I certainly tried to when I was younger, but your grandfather wouldn't let me."

"Can you picture Samantha living the kind of life you've led?"

"No, and more power to her. She has more in her future than organizing charity balls and seeing how many times a week she can get herself mentioned in the society pages. And what you've failed to realize is that her attitude is a plus, not a minus."

Pierce looked at his grandmother. "I don't want to be in love with her. We'll end up making each other miserable. I've seen too many of my friends marry women they shouldn't have with disastrous consequences."

"You're not like any of your friends, and none of their wives are like Samantha. Talk to her. You've got to get this settled or you might both end up doing something you'll regret."

"She doesn't want to talk to me. I tried this morning."

"So that's it, then? She didn't want to talk to you this morning and that's the end of it? She's in love with you, for heaven's sake."

"I know that," Pierce said softly as he left the table and walked over to the window, staring out at the ocean. "Samantha is the most open, honest women I've ever met. There's nothing coy about her. She feels what she feels. She can accept me for what I am, but I can't seem to do the same for her."

"If you think you're going to forget about her just because she's out of your life, you're wrong."

"Maybe. Maybe not."

Olivia shook her head. Men could be so obtuse at times.

Pierce walked over to his grandmother and kissed the top of her head. "I'm not very hungry this morning. I'll see you later."

He left the breakfast room and went into the hall. A maid was there, dusting. "Amy?"

She looked up.

"When Mr. von Schmidt comes downstairs, tell him I'd like to speak with him."

"He's gone already."

"What?" he asked sharply.

"He left right after Miss English.

A feeling of foreboding crept down Pierce's spine. Something was wrong. "How long after Miss English left was it before he followed her?"

"Only a minute or two. It was right after you and your grandmother went into the breakfast room."

Pierce strode into the library to get his keys and started out the front door, but stopped and went back into the library to make a call. "Come on, come on," he muttered impatiently when the information operator failed to answer by the second ring.

"What city, please?"

"Boston."

"May I help you?"

"I want the number for Harriet Fishbain."

There was a brief pause, and then a recorded voice gave him the number. He quickly dialed it and breathed a sigh of relief when Harriet answered the phone. "Hello, Harriet. This is Pierce Westcott."

"Oh, hello—"

"I don't have time to explain, but I want you to do me a favor. Go to Samantha's house and wait for her. As soon as she gets in, call me on my car phone." He gave her the number. "All right?"

"Sure, but—"

"She left here about half an hour ago, so she should be getting to Boston in another ninety minutes."

"I don't think so."

"Why?"

"She has a client in Westchester she was going to drop some papers off with."

"Westchester? That's quite a bit out of her way."

"No, not really. She was taking the scenic route home anyway."

"You mean she's not using the expressway?"

"That's right."

Pierce thought quickly. "Do you know who the client is she's going to see?"

"Sure."

"Call his house and leave a message for Sam to wait there for me. What's the address?"

Harriet gave it to him.

"You know it by heart?"

"No, but I prepared a bill yesterday that I forgot to mail. It's on my kitchen table."

"Is that the right address? Did you transpose the numbers?"

"Oh, ye of little faith. It's right. I double-check everything lately."

"Thanks, Harriet. I'll see you later."

He tossed the phone back in its cradle and ran out to his car.

About ten miles away, Samantha turned off of the highway and onto the quiet two-lane road that went to Westchester. It was a nice change of pace to be able to go for a drive without the urgency of having to be somewhere by a certain time.

She tried to pay attention to the passing scenery and enjoy some of the quiet towns she drove through, but it was difficult to block out her thoughts. It was easy to say that things would get better with time, but the fact was that she'd managed to fall in love with a man she knew she shouldn't, and now she was going to have to learn to live without him. It wasn't Pierce's fault. He'd been completely honest with her. It was no one's fault but her own. But she couldn't even be too hard on herself. Sometimes things happened over which one had no control. Pierce had happened to her.

She found the Caldwell house on a cosy suburban street and walked up to the door, file in hand. A man wearing a suit answered and smiled at her. "Miss English?"

"That's right."

"My wife's been expecting you." He turned and called his wife's name. "Sarah!" When there was no answer, he shook his head. "She's been on the phone all morning. In another five minutes we're going to be late for church."

Samantha handed him the file. "She knows what's in here. I've listed the names of the contacts I made on her behalf, and who I think she should contact on her own. The adoption agency who handled Sarah's adoption when she was a baby is willing to forward a letter from Sarah to her mother if Sarah makes the request in person, but after that it's up to Sarah's mother. If she doesn't want to meet Sarah, there's not much else we can do."

"I'll tell her. Thank you, Miss English."

"You're welcome. Wish her good luck for me."

She got back into her Jeep and headed for Boston, again over narrow back roads that rarely saw anything but local traffic anymore. It was like driving right into a picture postcard, with the single lane wooden bridges, some of them covered, all of them looking cared for.

As Sam stopped in front of a narrow bridge to allow another car to finish crossing, she noticed that she had to press on her brake pedal a little harder than usual to come to a full stop, and made a mental note to have that checked tomorrow.

A moment later she continued on her way, picking up speed and letting the wind whip her hair. She loved the sense of freedom being in the open like this gave her.

As she was leaning over to turn on the radio she glanced in the rearview mirror and spotted what looked like Albert von Schmidt's car behind her. "What on earth...?" she wondered aloud as she straightened without turning on the radio, curious but not yet worried. She slowed down, thinking he might want to catch up with her, but he slowed down, too. She slowed down even further, finally pulling over to the side of the road and stopping—with another hard push on her brake pedal. The other car did the same. Ordinarily, in a case such as this, Samantha would have gone back to the car to find out what was going on, but not this time. Her instincts told her to get out of there and get out fast. If it was von Schmidt, he had to have a reason for following her. How much did he suspect? How much did he know?

Samantha jammed her foot on the gas and, with her tires firing the roadside gravel behind them, shot off the shoulder and onto the road. The other car wasn't expecting it and fell behind at first, but quickly got closer. Samantha couldn't go much faster for fear she'd meet another car coming toward her head-on on the narrow road, but she did the best she could under the circumstances. It was strange, but she wasn't afraid yet. She had to concentrate too hard on her driving for anything to interfere. She saw one of those wooden bridges coming up and mentally crossed her fingers that no one else was trying to cross it. When she got closer, she sighed in relief. It was clear. She could tell from the sound as well as the feel of the car under her when she was on the bridge. Suddenly there was an explosion. One of her tires had blown up! The steering wheel jerked uncontrollably to the right in a spot where there was no room for error. Samantha watched with a sort of calm horror as her right headlight crashed through the fragile railing. Splintered wood flew all around her. The Jeep listed to the right as that side went off the bridge and started into an almost slow-motion roll as it became airborne.

Samantha was strangely clearheaded. She knew only that when she hit the water it couldn't be with the Jeep or she wouldn't survive. Standing on the seat, she pushed off with her feet and hit the water perhaps a second later, just a few feet from the Jeep, which landed upside down and sank like a stone, sending a geyser of water into the air and bubbles gurgling to the surface.

As Sam treaded water, she heard the other car stop on the bridge above her. She swam farther under it, trying desperately to keep out of sight. A car door opened. Footsteps sounded on the wood above her. A single pair. They stopped. It seemed like forever before they moved back to the car. The door closed. The car pulled away slowly, crossing the bridge and continuing down the road when it got to the other side.

Samantha made it to an embankment not far from where she was and pulled herself onto the grass, lying on her back, still shielded by the bridge above her, her hand over her pounding heart, her eyes closed. Her breath came in short, sharp gasps. She was alive. She was alive.

There was a great gulp where her car was. Sam opened her eyes and looked, then mentally corrected herself. Where her car *used* to be. She rose on her elbows and looked around. All was quiet. Apparently no one had seen what happened because no one had come to her rescue.

She sat up the rest of the way and an uncontrollable wave of shivering fingered its way through her soaked body. That had been so close. So horribly close. And it told her more than anything else that she was on the right track. She knew without any mechanic telling her that her brakes had been tampered with. And the way her tire had blown out was far from normal. It was as if it had exploded.

She should have gone back into the water to look at her car, but she just couldn't. It was murky and cold, and she couldn't bring herself to go back in there voluntarily.

Climbing to her feet, she pushed her wet hair out of her face and stood still for a moment as dizziness washed over her. She reached up and touched her forehead, then looked at her fingers. There was blood. She didn't remember bumping her head on anything, but she obviously had, and it was beginning to throb. A tear spilled down her already damp cheek, and she dashed it away with a shaking hand, annoyed by her weakness.

On wobbling legs she made her way up the hill and onto the bridge. As she stood at the spot where her car had gone over, they wobbled even more. She could so easily have been killed. Her suitcase had apparently burst open on impact, and its contents floated on the surface of the water.

She retraced her car's path before the tire had exploded to see if there was a nail or anything that would have caused it. She found a small battered metal case with what was left of an antenna hanging limply from it. A radio receiver. Could that be what blew out the tire? She picked it up and put it in her wet pocket, not sure it had any bearing on her accident, but unwilling to leave it behind.

She must be getting close to scare von Schmidt into attempting murder.

Murder. Another shiver went through her at the thought of how close von Schmidt had come to succeeding. And here she was, stuck out in the middle of nowhere with no car and no way to get home except walking.

Pierce quickly traveled the back roads along the only route he thought Samantha could have taken, his eyes everywhere, trying to find something, anything, out of place, and praying he wouldn't.

When he got to a bridge with a smashed railing, he stopped and sat in his car for a moment, a strange sense of foreboding filling him as it had earlier at the house. He slowly got out of his car and walked over to the gash, fingering the splintered wood. His gaze reluctantly went to the water where he saw clothes floating. Samantha's clothes. The suit she'd worn the day before to Jayne's wedding. An unsinkable tube of shampoo.

"Oh, my God," he whispered hoarsely. "Samantha." Half running, half sliding, he made his way down the embankment to the water's edge and looked for any sign of life. There was nothing. He couldn't even tell where the car was in the murky water.

Samantha had walked about two hundred yards when an old flatbed truck rattled past her and then stopped. Samantha ran up to the window. "Where are you going?"

The old man looked her over as though not quite sure whether he could trust her. She was a mess. "Boston."

"May I have a ride? I'll pay you if you can take me straight to my house. I'm afraid I haven't any money on me..."

He unsmilingly jerked his head toward the open-air rear of the truck. "Climb in back there. I'll take you as far as I'm going and after that you're on your own. Don't want your money."

Samantha could have kissed him. "Thank you."

"No need," he said gruffly.

As she climbed into the back she spotted a car stopped on the bridge in the distance. She narrowed her eyes in an effort to see better. It looked like Pierce's car. Had he come after her?

She quickly jumped off the back of the truck as it pulled out, and tried to run back to the bridge, but her head wouldn't let her. She had to slow down. The closer she got, the more sure she was that it was Pierce's car. But there was no one in it. Then she looked over the bridge railing and saw Pierce standing on the embankment. Relief flooded through her. "Pierce!"

He looked up at her in disbelief. "Samantha?" he said hoarsely. "Samantha!" He ran up to where she was standing and pulled her tightly into his arms. "Are you all right?" He held her away from him and looked at her blood-streaked face. "Of course you're not all right. What happened?" He pulled her back into his arms and buried his face in her hair. "I thought you were gone. I thought I'd lost you." He cupped her face in his hands and looked at her again, his eyes moving over each and every feature and resting there, memorizing her. His hand gently pushed her damp hair away from her injured forehead. "How did this happen?"

Her eyes went to the destroyed railing, and she shivered at the thought of what had almost happened to her. "My car went off the bridge. It's still there in the water somewhere."

Pierce's gaze went to the same spot. "My God." They were silent for a moment as Pierce rested his mouth against her hair. "How did it happen?" he asked quietly.

"I'm not sure, but I have an idea. Von Schmidt was following me. I didn't notice his car until a few miles before I got to this bridge. My brakes had been giving me a little trouble, but I forgot about them when I started speeding to get away from him. Then, when I got to this bridge, my tire suddenly blew out. I couldn't stop. I couldn't steer." She pulled the metal radio receiver out of her pocket. "I think this has something to do with it. I think it also explains why it took von Schmidt so long to come in last night. He was tampering with my car."

The muscle in his jaw moved. "I'll kill that son of a—"

Samantha put her hand on his arm. "I appreciate the sentiment." She closed her eyes for a moment against the headache that was starting to pound behind her eyes. "Can you get me to a police station? I think I have enough evidence for them to do something about von Schmidt. He's obviously nervous about something. We're talking about attempted murder here."

"First you're going to see a doctor. Then we'll worry about the police."

"But—"

"Doctor first." He raised her face to his. "Are you hurt anywhere else?"

"No."

He looked at her skeptically.

"Really."

Pierce helped her into his car and then climbed into the driver's seat. He looked at her pale profile as he put the Jaguar into gear. All he could think about was how close he had come to losing her. Suddenly the differences between them faded into insignificance.

Sam, oblivious to Pierce's look, leaned back in her seat with a sigh and closed her eyes. Pierce's warm hand suddenly covered hers. A soft smile touched Sam's mouth as she turned her hand over to clasp his. "What is it about you," she said quietly, her eyes still closed, "that makes me feel so safe?"

Pierce squeezed her hand but said nothing. It was strange how just one incident could take what appeared to be a jumbled mess and turn it into something amazingly simple.

They drove straight to his house in Boston. Pierce had her take off her still-wet clothes and change into one of his shirts after she'd showered the dirt from her hair and body.

He stood in the doorway of the bedroom, his shoulder leaning against the frame, and watched her as she fastened the last button on the shirt. "The doctor will be here in a few minutes."

"You know one who still makes house calls?"

Pierce ignored that as he came farther into the room and turned down the bed. "Get in."

He didn't have to ask twice. Samantha slid with a sigh between the sheets and let her head sink into the pillow. Pierce pulled the covers up around her and then sat watching her.

"You keep staring at me."

"Do I?"

"You're making me self-conscious."

"Can't be done." Pierce leaned over and kissed her hair. "I'll bring the doctor in as soon as he gets here."

"What about the police?"

"I've already called them. You don't even have to think about the case anymore. You're out of it."

Samantha sighed. "Good."

"Now, you, young lady, get some sleep."

She didn't need to be coaxed. After so many nights of only a few hours of sleep here and there, she fell into a deep and dreamless state almost instantly, and didn't even wake when the doctor came and examined her.

Pierce went into the room that served him both as library and office and poured himself a Scotch. Then he went back into the bedroom and sat in a chair next to the bed to watch the woman sleeping there.

"Pierce?" Samantha said softly from the bed.

He moved closer. "Hi, there."

"What time is it?"

"I don't know. It's night, though."

"How long have I been sleeping?"

"Hours. How's your head?"

"Fine."

Pierce sat on the edge of the bed and pushed her hair away from her face.

Sam tried to sit up. "I have to call the police."

Pierce pressed her gently back against the pillow. "We already went through that, darling."

"And the receiver?"

"They have it."

"Did they look at it? What is it? What did they say?"

"Nothing yet. They pulled your car out of the water a short time ago, and they'll call us as soon as someone has looked it over."

"Did you tell them about von Schmidt's meeting tomorrow night? Are they going to have him followed?"

"The police are taking care of everything, Sam. Stop thinking about it. Just relax."

"But—"

"No 'buts.' Just do as you're told."

Her eyes met his. "I don't do that very well."

"Then practice."

"Yes, sir."

Pierce leaned slowly forward and kissed her lips, then lifted his head and gazed down at her.

Samantha tried to read his thoughts, but couldn't.

He kissed her again. Samantha's arms went around his neck, pulling him closer. Pierce lowered himself on top of her, his mouth searching hers, his tongue probing the moist depths, getting to know the taste of her. He raised himself slightly so that he could get his hand into the V opening of the shirt she was wearing. His shirt. It was all she had on. As he opened the shirt, button by slow button, his mouth followed his fingers down her body. When he opened the last button, he softly moved his mouth back and forth over her abdomen.

Samantha lay there with her eyes closed, not moving. Just enjoying the incredible awareness his touch stirred in her. Relishing each kiss, each breath against her sensitized skin. She opened her eyes when she felt Pierce leave the bed and stand up, and she watched as he undressed. She could see in the moonlight that he was beautiful, with the solid, lean body of an athlete, the muscles clearly defined.

Again his body covered hers, but this time he rolled onto his side and took Samantha with him so that they lay facing one another. His forehead rested against hers as his hand cupped the back of her head. Samantha kissed his mouth slowly, then moved so that their lips were almost but not quite touching. Samantha started to say something, but Pierce stopped her. "Don't talk. We always get into trouble when we talk."

He wrapped his arm farther around Samantha and pulled her body against his. His hand tangled in her hair and drew her mouth to his as he turned his body again and pressed her back into the bed. His hand slid down her side and along her thigh, then came back up slowly and began gently stroking her. Samantha's mouth left his at the unexpectedness of the feelings that surged through her, her back arched, her throat vulnerable. His mouth moved down her neck to her breast and delicately teased her already erect nipple.

Samantha inhaled sharply, overwhelmed by the power of what was happening to her body. A body that seemed to take on a life of its own under his gentle and sure ministrations.

Somewhere in the back of her mind she heard the sound of a doorbell, but it didn't register. There wasn't any room in her senses for anything outside what Pierce was doing to her.

But whoever was there was persistent, and it began to intrude. Pierce covered Sam's body with his own. "Maybe if we ignore it, it'll go away."

She moved her hands slowly down his muscled shoulders to his thighs and held him tightly against her.

The doorbell rang again and again, refusing to be ignored.

Pierce rolled off of Samantha and lay on his back for a minute, his forearm over his eyes.

Samantha shivered in response to the sudden denial of what her body was clamoring for. Pierce protectively wrapped her in a sheet and pulled her into his arms, holding her close to him. "I'll be right back."

Her eyes lingered on his body as he put on his pants and shirt. Pierce leaned over and kissed her tenderly on the mouth and again on the cheek, then left the room.

Samantha lay very still when he'd gone, staring at the ceiling. She was as unhappy as she'd ever been. Everything would have been just fine if she'd never met him. But she had. And he'd made it clear that morning that there was no future for them.

So what was she doing making love to him?

A silent tear escaped from the corner of her eye. She was saying goodbye.

Pierce opened the door, and Sam quickly dashed away the tear and smiled at him. "Hello, again."

He sat on the edge of the bed and looked down at her. "I'm going to have to leave for an hour or so. Will you be all right here alone?"

"Of course. Where are you going?"

He kissed her cheek. "There's nothing for you to concern yourself with. And when I get back we'll pick up where we left off."

Samantha wrapped her arms around his neck and pulled his mouth to hers.

"Then again," he said quietly, kissing her again, "perhaps we'll start all over again." He walked to the door, but turned back to her. "Are you all right? You're very quiet."

"I'm fine. Goodbye, Pierce."

He hesitated a moment longer. "I'll see you in a little while."

As soon as the door had closed behind him, Samantha sat up slowly and put her hand to her head. It didn't hurt as much as she'd expected. She was wearing one of Pierce's shirts, and she just left it on and went into the bathroom where her jeans were hung on a towel rack. They were dry, but stiff. She put them on and then found her shoes, which were also stiff.

She opened the bedroom door and listened for a moment. It was silent, so Pierce must have left. She went back into the bedroom. Her eyes fell on a pad and pen by the telephone. Picking up the pen, she quickly scribbled a note to Pierce. "I'm going home. Please don't worry about me anymore. Thanks for all your help. Sam." When she read it back, it seemed stilted and formal. There wasn't a single word of what she was feeling. But she left it that way.

A moment later she walked out the front door and went to the first busy street corner where she hailed a taxi and headed for her house.

Chapter Nine

When the cab stopped in front of Sam's house, the first thing she noticed was that Harriet's car was parked there. Sam leaned forward and touched the driver on the shoulder. "I have to go inside to get some money. I'll be right back."

The door was unlocked. Sam opened it and quickly walked straight through to her office for some money. "Harriet," she called out, "it's me, Sam. I just have to pay the taxi. Wait until you hear what happened to me today." She found the money and ran back out to the taxi with it, then returned to the house, closing the door after her and walking into the living room. "Harriet?" Sam stopped and listened. There was no noise. "Harriet?"

"Miss English, how nice of you to join us." She raised her eyes to find Albert von Schmidt standing in the doorway of her kitchen. Sam's heart stopped for a moment and then started again.

"What are you doing here? Where's Harriet? What have you done with her?"

"Your secretary—and your client, as a matter of fact—are just fine, and if you'll simply step in here you'll see that for yourself."

Samantha moved forward tentatively, turning sideways when she got to the doorway so she wouldn't have to touch von Schmidt. Both Harriet and Sidney sat blindfolded in the kitchen. Their hands and feet were bound. When Sam would have run to them, von Schmidt grabbed her arm. "Oh, no, Miss English. I think not."

Samantha didn't struggle, but glared at the hand he held her with. "Let go of me."

"You are hardly in a position to give me orders. Relax, dear." He looked her up and down. "You're looking well considering all you went through earlier. I must admit—" he moved a finger suggestively on her arm, sending a distasteful shiver through her "—that I'm rather pleased—if surprised—to see you."

Samantha was only half listening to him. Her eyes moved around the room looking for a way out. Any way out.

Von Schmidt followed her gaze. "Forget it, Samantha. You'll be doing as I tell you from now on."

"What about Harriet and Sidney?"

"They can just make themselves comfortable. My friend—" he gestured to a darkened corner of the room where a man whose face she couldn't identify sat with a gun pointed at her "—will be staying here with them while you and I take a trip. If you try to run away from me, your friends will be killed. By the same token, when I call here, if I don't hear my friend's voice at the other end of the line, you will be eliminated without hesitation.''

"And when we get to where we're going what happens to everyone?''

"First of all, we're going to Zurich. I can tell you that quite freely because by the time anyone else finds out where we are, I shall be long gone. And when we get there, if all goes well, all three of you will be set free.''

Samantha didn't believe him, but she didn't have any choice. "What about the technology information you're selling? You don't have it yet.''

"But I do. The realization that you'd picked up my messages moved things up a little.'' He looked at his watch and then at Samantha. "I strongly suggest you change your clothes, Miss English. And dress comfortably. It's a long flight. And don't try anything while you're upstairs, because if you do your friends here will pay dearly, I promise you.''

Samantha left the kitchen and went upstairs to her bedroom. Her mind was whirling as she changed her clothes, not really paying attention to the full yellow skirt and blouse she put on, but trying desperately to think of a way to get in touch with Pierce. How could she have been so stupid as to leave his house the way she had? It had never even occurred to her that von Schmidt would be here.

And what if Pierce showed up here later looking for her? He just might. She hadn't thought of that. He'd be walking right into the middle of something.

There was a sharp knock on her door. "Come, come, Miss English. We haven't much time to catch our flight.''

"I'm almost ready." Samantha walked quickly to
her dresser and opened the bottom drawer. There was
a small flashlight she kept for emergencies. She
jammed it into her skirt pocket. Straightening, she
caught a glimpse of herself in the mirror. Her hair was
a mass of uncombed curls; her cheeks were flushed
with fear. She took a deep breath and went to the
door. "I'm ready."

The German looked her up and down. "So you are.
We'll be on our way now."

He went into the kitchen and spoke briefly with the
shadowed man, then came back to Samantha.
"Now."

She took a last look at Harriet and Sidney, silently
wishing them well, and followed von Schmidt out the
front door. When she got to the bottom step, she
turned on the flashlight and dropped it on the grass
next to the sidewalk. Von Schmidt never looked back.

When Pierce got back to his house, he quickly
walked into the bedroom, only to find it empty.
"Sam?" he called, looking around the room. "Sam?"
He opened the closed bathroom door. His eyes fell on
the towel rack where he'd put her clothes to dry. Her
blouse was still there, but her jeans were gone. He
slammed his fist against the door and turned to leave.
His glance fell on the note Sam had written. Pierce
picked it up and read it through once and then again.

"Samantha English," he said in a low voice, "when
I get my hands on you, so help me..." He jammed the
note into his pocket and went out to his car. As angry
as he was, it took him less than ten minutes to get to
her house. He saw Harriet's car parked in front and
suddenly realized that he'd told her earlier to sit by the

phone and wait for Sam, but had forgotten to call her when he'd found Sam.

As he strode down the sidewalk, he saw something shining up at him. He picked up the flashlight and frowned at it as he pressed the button to turn it off. What on earth was this doing out here? With a shake of his head he started up the steps, but stopped and again studied the flashlight. The last time he'd seen one of these, Samantha had been in trouble. Was this her way of telling him she was in trouble again?

Not taking any chances, Pierce retraced his steps and went quietly around to the back of the house, looking in the lighted windows as he went. When he got to the kitchen windows, he stopped. Harriet and a man were sitting blindfolded and bound while another man nervously paced up and down. A gun sat on the counter, never too far from the pacing man's fingertips.

Pierce moved away from the window and leaned his back against the wall. What now? Where was Sam? Who else was in the house?

Pierce picked up a handful of small rocks, then walked across the dark yard and tossed a few against the window. The man stopped his pacing, picked up his gun and looked out the window. Pierce backed even farther into the shadows. When the man turned his head to say something to Harriet and the man with her, Pierce tossed some more gravel. This time the man looked more closely. Pierce moved around by the back door, his back flat against the wall, and waited. Sure enough, a moment later the door slowly opened. Pierce watched as the barrel of the gun poked through first, slowly followed by the hand holding it. Pierce raised his arm and then suddenly brought the side of his hand down on the man's arm as hard as he could. The gun fired and then fell to the ground. Pierce struggled briefly with the man, surprised at how easily the fellow was subdued, and caught him once on the jaw, completely knocking him out.

"Harriet," he called out, "are you all right?"

"Mr. Westcott?" she said in disbelief. "Is that really you?"

Pierce retrieved the gun and then cut Harriet loose. She undid her own blindfold while Pierce cut the rope around the man's hands. "You must be Sidney Poondorken," Pierce said as he straightened. "Where's Sam?" he asked without waiting for Sidney to answer.

"Von Schmidt has her."

"What do you mean 'has her'? Has her where?"

"He said something about taking her to Zurich. And he's going to be calling here every so often to make sure his accomplice still has things under control."

"And what happens if the accomplice doesn't answer?"

"Then Sam is in trouble."

Pierce stepped back into the doorway, grabbed the man by his shirt collar and dragged him inside. As he did, the man's hat fell off and long brown hair spilled out. Sidney's eyes widened. "Annette?"

The woman moaned and opened her eyes.

Sidney knelt beside her. "Annette? You?"

She turned her face away from his.

Pierce looked at him curiously. "Who is she?"

"She was my assistant at Amerigroup."

Pierce stood looking unsympathetically down at her. "You were stealing technology for von Schmidt?"

"I don't have to tell you anything."

"Of course you don't. But you're going to. And when your friend von Schmidt calls to see if everything is in order, you're going to tell him that everything is fine."

"And if I don't?"

Pierce smiled at her, and it was one of the most threatening expressions Harriet had ever seen. "Let's just say that I wouldn't want to be you if anything happens to Samantha."

The woman swallowed and tried to sit up, but Pierce put his foot on her shoulder and held her down. "Do you understand what I'm saying to you?" he asked evenly.

She nodded.

"Good." He lifted his foot and allowed her to stand. "Sidney, tie her to the chair. Harriet, tell me everything you overheard. Everything."

Harriet thought for a moment. "There really wasn't much. He said he already had what he intended to sell and that he was taking Sam to Zurich with him."

"How long ago did they leave for the airport?"

Harriet shook her head. "I can't really say because I couldn't see my watch, but it seems like it's been at least two hours—maybe even three."

He turned to Sidney's ex-assistant. "What airline were they taking?"

"I don't know." Pierce moved to stand in front of her, but she shook her head. "I honestly don't know. I don't even know what airport they left from."

Pierce sighed. "Do you know who von Schmidt is meeting in Zurich?"

"No one."

"No one?"

"Zurich isn't his final destination."

"And what is?"

"Venice. They'll be taking a train from Zurich to Venice. It's loaded with tourists this time of year. A few more will never be noticed."

Pierce didn't know whether to believe her or not, but then decided lying at this point wouldn't do her any good. She was caught. Sidney stood next to him. "What are you going to do now? Call the police?"

"The police are fine for Annette, but they can't help us with von Schmidt." He thought for a moment. "If we can find out what flight they took, the Swiss police could nab von Schmidt when he gets off the plane in Zurich."

Sidney suddenly turned to Annette. "What is it that you gave von Schmidt?"

Annette didn't say anything.

"It's over, you know," he said quietly, pushing his glasses up on his nose. "You might as well come clean. Your secrets can't help you anymore."

Annette studied her hands. "He has the laser research you were working on."

"What's she talking about?" Pierce asked.

Sidney turned to Pierce. "You've heard of Star Wars?"

"Of course."

"Well, I've been working on a technique using lasers rather than missiles to defuse, or blow up, any foreign objects that enter United States airspace. It hasn't been tested yet, but it shows a great deal of promise."

"And that's what von Schmidt has?"

"I'm afraid so."

"This isn't some penny-ante theft. The stakes are high and the penalties for getting caught are severe. And Sam's right in the middle of it." Pierce thought for a moment. "Sidney, I want you to stay here with Annette and make sure she says all the right things when von Schmidt calls. Harriet, I want you to call the police here and in Zurich. Then I want you to get in touch with whatever government agency handles this kind of thing and tell them exactly what's happening."

"What about you?"

"I'm catching the first plane to Zurich I can get on. If the Swiss can catch them when they get off the plane, it'll be all over. If not, I'll be going on to Venice after them. Either way, tell whoever you talk with in the government to meet me at the airport."

"I should be coming with you," Sidney told him.

"Not this time."

Sidney caught Pierce's arm. "You don't understand. Miss English is in this trouble because of me. I have to help. I have to."

A corner of Pierce's mouth lifted. "You are helping by staying here. Someone has to. Samantha is in this trouble because of herself, not you. Trouble follows her around as though she were a magnet. I've never seen anything like it."

Harriet smiled knowingly. "And you love her."

"And I love her," he admitted, "though I don't know if it's because of the way she is or despite it. Make those calls, Harriet. I'll be in touch as soon as I find something out."

Samantha watched out the window as the big jet she was on narrowed the distance between itself and earth on its approach to the Zurich airport. Von Schmidt sat calmly next to her. "I see we're almost there."

"May I leave after we've landed?"

"No."

"But you said . . ."

"I wasn't at all specific about when I'd be letting you go. I suppose it'll be when you're no longer useful to me."

The jet touched down and von Schmidt, with his hand under her arm, led her off the jet, through customs and out of the terminal. There was no need to go to baggage claim since the only thing they had between them was a briefcase, and he'd kept that with him on the plane.

They got into a taxi, and the taxi took them straight to a railroad station. Von Schmidt purchased two tickets, showed them briefly to a man who inquired as they climbed aboard, and led her to a private cubicle with two long couches. Samantha sat down in silence and stared out the window.

"There's no need to look so gloomy," von Schmidt told her. "You're going to a lovely place. Try to think of it as a little vacation."

Samantha looked him in the eye. "You're crazy if you think you're going to get away with this."

"But I already have gotten away with it, don't you see? The hard part's over with. No one questioned the falsified passports. No one knows who we really are or even where we're going. And traveling on a train like this from Switzerland into Italy, passports frequently aren't even checked."

Samantha sighed and looked out the window as the train began to slowly pull out of the station. "Are you sure your friend isn't going to hurt Sidney or my secretary?"

"As long as they keep their blindfolds on there'll be no need to hurt anyone."

Samantha watched the passing scenery. It was beautiful once they were away from the station. The hills turned into mountains. Carpets of green grass surrounded hillside chalets, all obviously well-tended with flowers and fresh paint. Crystal-clear lakes with expensive vacation retreats were set among pines.

That changed when they got into Italy. Suddenly the lawns weren't so well-tended. Paint peeled from the houses, and there was litter along the tracks and sometimes on the hills. Hours after they'd started out, the train pulled into another station. The sign on the front said *Milano*.

Von Schmidt rose as soon as the train came to a halt. "Come on," he said impatiently.

"Where are we going?"

"Don't ask questions. Just move it. We don't have much time."

Samantha walked quickly behind him through the huge station. There were at least twelve trains stopped on parallel tracks, all of them noisy, ready to leave. Sam got bumped around by people passing them or running in the opposite direction.

Von Schmidt led her to a telephone and dialed a series of numbers; then he leaned back and waited, his eyes on Samantha. "Hello, my friend. Are things in order?" He listened to the answer. "Very good. I'll be in touch." Then he hung up. "Lucky for you, Miss English. We can be on our way." They climbed onto another train, this one, if the sign was to be believed, bound for *Venezia*, or Venice.

Samantha looked at the German curiously as he seated himself across from her once again. "Venice?"

"Not my choice, believe me."

"I didn't think so." He didn't look like the type who would enjoy a trip to Venice. "What exactly is it that you're selling this time?"

"That's none of your concern."

"I'm not concerned. I'm merely curious. You're almost home free now. There's no reason not to tell me."

Von Schmidt just smiled at her and looked out the window as the train pulled out of the Milan station.

Samantha settled back in her seat with a sigh and waited. She'd apparently been wasting her time by leaving a clue for Pierce. Judging from the phone call von Schmidt had just made, he apparently hadn't even shown up. All was as it had been when she'd left.

So now what was she going to do? She couldn't run away because of Harriet and Sidney. She couldn't do anything to von Schmidt for the same reason. She studied his profile. What an awful man.

He in turn looked at her. "You know, my beautiful Samantha, it's too bad."

"What is?"

"That we couldn't have met under other circumstances." His eyes trailed over her slowly and suggestively. "I think we might have discovered that we have quite a bit in common."

Samantha's eyes didn't waver. "I don't think so."

"Going to save yourself for Westcott, are you?"

She said nothing.

"He might take you to bed, you know, but he certainly isn't going to marry you. You would never fit into his way of life."

"Mind your own business."

"Why? Speculation is so much more entertaining, don't you think? And we have several more hours to kill—if you'll pardon the expression—before we get to Venice."

"Then entertain yourself with silent speculation, will you? I don't want to hear it."

Von Schmidt smiled. "You might just change your mind about me yet, Samantha English. You know, with the money I'll be getting shortly, we could live a good life."

"By whose standards?"

Von Schmidt smiled at her thoughtfully, as though he hadn't heard her. "Yes, indeed, we could live a very good life."

Samantha looked at him steadily for a few moments, then turned her head and stared out the window. She didn't speak again until hours later when they arrived in Venice.

Chapter Ten

When Pierce got off the plane in Switzerland, there was no one there to meet him. Not knowing what had gone on since he'd left Boston, he found a phone and called Harriet.

"Thank heavens you called," she said as she took the phone away from Annette.

"Did the Swiss police arrest von Schmidt?"

"That's what I wanted to talk to you about. They didn't arrest anyone. There was no record of either Samantha or von Schmidt entering the country. If they went through customs there, they must have done it with different passports."

"Damn."

"And I didn't know who to call in our government, so I started by asking the police who to call. They said the FBI. I called the FBI and they told me to call another agency and so on and so on. I never did get any help."

"So I'm on my own."

"I have a call in now to the Pentagon, but no one has called me back. If nothing else, I'm hoping someone there can tell me which agency is the right one to contact."

"Well, keep trying, Harriet. I'm going to head for Venice now. I'll check with you again in a few hours."

Pierce hung up the phone and stood there for a minute. How in the hell was he going to find her on his own? He didn't know where to begin. Venice was a big place. A big, crowded place.

Samantha sat in the window seat of her room in von Schmidt's castello and looked out at the Grand Canal. Gondoliers, the ribbons on their flat-brimmed hats flapping, skillfully steered their tourist-packed gondolas under narrow and low bridges.

There was a knock on the door. A dead bolt slid back and von Schmidt walked in. "Hello, my dear. Lovely day, don't you think?"

Samantha just looked at him.

"I trust you slept well. The waters usually have a lulling effect on me."

Samantha went back to gazing out the window.

"It won't do you any good to ignore me, you know. I'm not going away. At least not permanently. Your part in this should be over soon, though."

Sam turned back to him. "Are you going to let me go?"

He lifted her hair and let it slip silkily through his fingers. "You can come with me when this is all over. Think about it. The world will be yours."

Sam moved away from him. "Don't touch me."

Von Schmidt's hand dropped. Without saying anything else, he left the room. Sam heard him lock the door and then listened as his footsteps disappeared down the hall.

She reached out and clasped one of the black iron bars that imprisoned the window. She couldn't explain why, but she had a feeling von Schmidt wasn't going to let her go. She knew too much. Perhaps he'd already taken care of Harriet and Sidney. He'd called several times, but not once had he let her speak with them.

A water taxi pulled up in front of the castello and its engine idled. Sam leaned forward, pressing the sides of her face against the bars, to see what was going on. Von Schmidt stepped out and took the offered hand of the motor taxi man as he climbed aboard. "Piazza San Marco. Avanti," she heard him say.

She watched until the motor taxi was out of sight, then leaned back, frustrated beyond belief at her utter helplessness. He was obviously going to make the deal, and there wasn't a thing she could do about it.

Another gondola went by. She noticed it particularly because there was only one passenger. A man. Lone men never went on gondolas. There was something about him. She narrowed her eyes and tried to get a better look. It was hard to see in the bright sunlight. Then he turned his head just so, and Samantha gasped. "Pierce." Then she yelled loudly, "Pierce! Pierce! Up here!"

Pierce at first thought he was imagining he heard Sam's voice. "Stop!" he called to the gondolier, who immediately obeyed.

"Pierce!"

He turned and looked up and saw an arm waving at him through some black iron bars from two floors above the water. He signaled the gondolier to take him to the castello entrance, which the man did. He stayed in the gondola and looked up at Sam. "Are you all right?"

"I'm fine. What about Harriet and Sidney?"

"They're fine, too."

"What about the man who was holding them?"

"It was a woman, Sidney's assistant at Amerigroup."

"A woman? Not the new head of research and development?"

"That's right. Dropping the flashlight was a big help. Thanks."

Sam smiled, and his heart leaped. She was really here. He could hardly believe he'd found her.

"Is von Schmidt with you?"

"No. He just went to the Piazza San Marco. I think he's winding up his deal."

"Is there anyone there with you?"

"Not in my room, but I don't know about the rest of the castello. I'm locked in."

He left the gondola and turned to the man in it. "Wait."

The gondolier looked at him curiously.

"Wait here, please. You understand?"

The man nodded, and Pierce walked cautiously into the unlocked castello. It was dark and damp inside. Stone stairs covered in mildewed carpeting led to the upper level. He took them two at a time, then stopped at the top and looked up and down the hallway. Still no sign of anyone. "Samantha?" he called softly.

"In here."

He went to the door and looked it over. There was an ancient dead bolt lock on the outside. He slid it over and opened the door. Samantha flew into his arms. Arms that Pierce wrapped tightly around her. For the second time in days, he buried his face in her hair, amazed at the strength of his feelings for her. "Samantha English," he said softly, "if you ever do anything like this again, so help me I'll lock you in a padded cell."

Samantha moved away from him. Her eyes looked into his. "I'm sorry. I seem to keep dragging you into the middle of things. I don't mean to. It just happens." Suddenly her eyes grew wider. "We have to get to the Piazza San Marco. I think von Schmidt is making his deal there."

"You aren't going anywhere near the Piazza," Pierce informed her.

"But . . ."

"No. I'll drop you off at my hotel and I want you to stay there."

"Pierce," she said quietly, "I appreciate the fact that you came after me more than I'll ever be able to express, but this thing with von Schmidt has nothing to do with you. I don't want you caught in the middle of a mess that I made."

"You're wrong." He gently touched her cheek. "Von Schmidt became my business the moment he tried to hurt you. He's not going to get away with this." He took her hand and pulled her along behind him. "Come on."

When they got to the gondola, Pierce climbed in first and then lifted Samantha in. "Hotel Danieli," he told the gondolier, who then pushed away from the castello and made his slow, graceful way down the canal. The Danieli was also on the Grand Canal, and not all that far from the castello. When the gondola stopped, it was by some stairs that led directly from the water to the hotel. Pierce helped Sam out and then looked at her threateningly. "I want you to go straight to my room and stay there. Ask for the key at the desk. I'll fill you in on everything as soon as I get back."

Samantha's blue eyes held his brown ones, but she made no promises. "Don't do anything crazy and get yourself hurt."

A corner of his mouth lifted, deepening the crease in his cheek. "You, of all people, Sam, should know how conservative I am." He turned back to the gondolier. "Piazza San Marco."

Sam watched as the gondolier poled the craft back into traffic. She couldn't let him do this alone. If anything happened to him, she'd never forgive herself. Sam walked into the elegant hotel and looked for another entrance. There had to be one with a walk for pedestrians. And there was. She went to the front desk and waited impatiently while the clerk finished with the person ahead of her. When he finally turned to her, his eyes grew appreciative. "Hello," he said in English, apparently knowing what nationality she was without having to ask.

"Hello. I need to know how to get to Piazza San Marco from here."

"It is a simple matter. You are very close. When you leave through that door—" he pointed to the one she'd been looking at "—turn right and then go straight. You'll have to cross two foot bridges. That will bring you to the Palace of the Doges. Turn right as soon as you get past that and you'll walk straight onto the piazza."

She smiled at him. "Thank you."

"It was very much my pleasure."

Samantha walked quickly outside. The walkway that ran alongside the canal was wide, but it had to be to accommodate the people. Samantha found herself dodging here and there to get past them, but sometimes there was nothing she could do but slow down, or stop altogether and wait for them to decide to move. Sometimes she got gently pushy and moved them whether they were ready to move or not. An elaborate palace loomed on her right. That must be the doge's one the clerk had mentioned. Sam walked around the corner of the building and found a long brick walkway with shops lining it. Farther along it suddenly and unexpectedly opened into a huge courtyard, surrounded on all sides by castellos. Several open-air cafés had been set up and were crowded with people. Small shops selling souvenirs were hidden between the pillars of most of the castellos on the ground floor. Samantha's eyes searched the mass of humanity for Pierce or von Schmidt, but she couldn't see either of them. It was impossible to see anything from where she was.

Near panic, Samantha looked around for something to stand on. Someone laughed from above her and she looked up. There was a lovely cathedral. Tourists hung out the windows. Samantha ran inside and straight past the ticket seller, who grabbed her by the arm and pulled her back. He said something in Italian and pointed to a hand-printed sign stating clearly that admittance was one thousand lire. Samantha looked at him in obvious distress. She reached into her skirt pockets and pulled them inside out so he could see that she had no money. "Per favore," she said, using her painfully limited Italian. "Please. Molto importante."

The man sighed and shook his head as though he hated himself for being such a pushover, but waved her through.

Samantha, in her enthusiasm, threw her arms around him and kissed his surprised cheek. "Grazie!" And she ran off in search of the stairs. She found them with very little trouble and ran up them two at a time, past some startled tourists. When she got to the top, she ran straight to the open windows and managed to get close enough to look out at the piazza. She could see the whole area. The person immediately next to her moved, giving her more room. She moved closer to the ledge and leaned out as her eyes began a methodical search of the mass of humanity below. Person by person, she eliminated them. Her gaze went to one of the cafés and searched it table by table. Nothing. Then she looked in the distance at the other café. It looked like von Schmidt at one of the tables, but he was too far away for her to be sure. Samantha looked at the tourists around her and saw one with a camera and a zoom lens. "Excuse me," she said politely, "do you speak English?"

"You bet."

"Would you mind if I borrowed your camera for a minute?"

He looked taken aback by her request.

"I'm not going to run off with it. I think I see someone I know, and I need to get a closer look. You can stand right behind me the whole time I have it."

Without saying anything, the man handed her the camera. Sam raised it to her eye and focused on the café. Sure enough, it was von Schmidt. Another man had just joined him. But there was no sign of Pierce yet. She spotted someone else, though. Sam handed the man back his camera. "Thanks. Would you do me one more favor?"

The poor man looked as though he couldn't believe he was having this conversation with a stranger, but was too nice to say no. "I guess. What?"

"Do you see that policeman down there headed for the doge's palace?"

He looked out the window and nodded. "About three hundred yards away."

"That's the one. I need you to get him and tell him to come to a table at the far café. Look through your camera."

The man did.

"Do you see the man sitting with his back to you wearing a tan suit?" No one else in the entire piazza had on a suit. Von Schmidt stood out.

"Yes. There's another man with him."

"That's the table I want the policeman to come to."

"All right."

"And please hurry."

He nodded, and they both went quickly down the steps.

When Sam got outside again, she looked around once more for Pierce without any luck at all. Wondering what on earth she was going to do, she started across the piazza toward von Schmidt. Surely he wouldn't do anything to her in public.

The walk seemed to take forever. She couldn't see von Schmidt at all until she was almost on top of him. She stood there waiting for the policeman to come, but he didn't. And then it looked as though von Schmidt and his friend were getting ready to leave. Sam had to do something. She quickly grabbed a bread stick from the table she was standing near, walked up behind von

Schmidt, and poked him in the back with it. Still seated, he looked at her over his shoulder. "Hello, Albert," she said pleasantly. "Don't move please, or this gun I have in your back might go off." Then she smiled at the man seated across from the German. "Do you speak English?"

"Yes."

"Good. Then we all understand one another."

The man looked at von Schmidt. "What's going on?"

"What's going on," Samantha explained, "is that we're going to wait here for a policeman, and then the two of you are going to be arrested."

Suddenly a waiter walked over to her, full of indignation. He grabbed the bread stick from her hand, waved it in her face and sputtered at her in furious and probably unrepeatable Italian. Samantha was left standing there wishing the earth would open up and swallow her whole. She smiled at the man with von Schmidt. "Hi there. Just kidding." But he wasn't amused. He pulled a real gun out of his jacket and aimed it at Sam. As she stood there frozen, waiting for the inevitable, someone suddenly knocked her out of the way almost at the same time as an explosion filled the air.

There was panic in the piazza. Screams filled the air as people ran, confusing things even more.

The body on top of Sam moved. For the first time she saw Pierce. He looked at her as though he wanted to strangle her. "What are you doing here? I *told* you to stay at the hotel."

She stood up too, brushing off her skirt. "I couldn't let you do my dirty work. This whole mess is my fault."

"You won't get any argument from me."

A policeman had grabbed von Schmidt's friend and had his hands already handcuffed. Samantha looked around. "Where's von Schmidt?"

Pierce looked too, spotting a running figure in a tan suit some distance ahead. "There he goes." Then he looked at Sam. "I don't suppose it would do any good for me to tell you to wait here."

"No."

"Come on, then." He grabbed her hand and they tore off through the people. It was like running through a maze. They lost sight of von Schmidt, but Pierce seemed to know where he was going. When they got to the Grand Canal, Pierce stopped and looked. Sam stood panting beside him.

"There he is!" she said excitedly as she spotted the tan suit climbing into a gondola several hundred yards away.

Pierce looked around for a water taxi but couldn't find one. He raced over to a gondola, dragging Sam behind him, and jumped in. The young man who owned it looked at them in surprise.

"Follow that gondola," Pierce ordered, pointing to the one disappearing around a corner. Then he looked at Samantha and shook his head. "I don't believe I just said that."

As the young man poled them into the canal, Pierce pressed Samantha onto a seat and sat next to her. "Do you speak English?" he asked the fellow.

"Little."

Pierce pulled out his wallet and removed half of its contents. He set it near the man. "If you can catch up with that gondola, I'll give you the rest of it."

The young man grinned and tipped his hat. "Yes, sir." And with that, they were off. Von Schmidt had a head start, but his gondolier wasn't half what theirs was. The young man had all but pulled alongside the other gondola as they reached von Schmidt's castello. Pierce leaped across the water separating them and landed squarely in von Schmidt's gondola, quickly wrestling him to the floor.

Samantha noticed for the first time a red stain on Pierce's white shirt and realized that he'd been hit by the bullet. Von Schmidt must have noticed the same thing, because he hit Pierce on his wounded arm. Pierce lost his grip for just a moment, but it was enough for von Schmidt to get up. He grabbed his briefcase and swung it at Pierce as Pierce got to his feet, missing his head by inches. While von Schmidt was off-balance, Pierce let fly with a powerful punch that knocked von Schmidt, briefcase and all, into the water.

The German went under and then came back up. "I can't swim," he yelled. "Help me."

Pierce took the gondolier's pole and set it in the water next to von Schmidt. The German grabbed it and started to climb back into the gondola, but Pierce blocked his way. "You wait there, von Schmidt. The police will be along in a minute." Then he sat down, clasping the wounded arm close to his side.

Samantha watched him, her heart in her eyes. "We have to get you to a doctor, Pierce."

Brown eyes met hers. "I don't need a doctor. I need a bodyguard," he said dryly.

She knew what he meant. Someone to protect him from her.

Pierce took out his wallet and tossed it to Sam. "Give him the rest of the money." Then he looked at the smiling young gondolier. "Grazie."

Sam gave him the money and put the wallet in her skirt pocket. She would have crossed to the other gondola, but there was too much distance between them. So what was new? "Are you sure you're all right?" she asked Pierce.

He winked reassuringly at her. "It's not bad."

"It's bleeding a lot."

Pierce dragged the sleeve of his uninjured arm across his perspiring forehead. "Where are the police?"

No sooner had he said the words than two water taxis carrying several uniformed men pulled alongside them. Pierce pointed out von Schmidt hanging onto the pole. The police pulled him in. "There's a briefcase down there that has to be recovered," he told another one. "It's important."

"We'll take care of it," the officer replied in good English; then he inclined his head toward Pierce's arm. "Come with us. We'll take you to a doctor."

Pierce climbed into the water taxi. Samantha stood there watching, not sure what to do. Pierce turned to her as though he'd read her thoughts. "Sam, go back to the hotel, and this time, for heaven's sake, *stay* there. Can you do that for me?"

"Yes," she said quietly.

"Promise?"

She nodded.

"I'll see you in a little while."

Sam watched as the water taxi disappeared into the distance. The young gondolier looked at her curiously. "Hotel?"

She nodded and sat down with a sigh. "Danieli."

Sam was so wrapped up in her thoughts that she didn't notice anything around her until they were at the hotel. The young man stepped out of the gondola and held out his hand to help her. She smiled her thanks.

"You need go fast again, you come geta Luigi."

Her smile grew. "Thank you, Luigi. We'll do that."

He grinned at her, bobbed his head a few times and climbed back in.

Samantha went into the hotel and to the front desk. The same clerk was there. "Did you find Piazza San Marco?"

"I certainly did. Your directions were perfect. May I please have the key to Pierce Westcott's room?"

"You are with him?" he asked.

"Sort of."

He took a key from a board behind him and handed it to her. "The room is on the fourth floor, overlooking the canal."

"Thank you." She saw the elevators, but decided to use the stairs instead. They weren't normal hotel stairs, but were wide and elegant as though people were expected to use them.

When she got to Pierce's room, she let herself in and then stood just inside the door and looked around. It didn't look occupied. There was no luggage. Everything was in its place.

She moved farther into the room. Night was falling. The sounds of the people below were getting quieter. Those who had come just for the day were leaving. Others had gone to their hotels to get ready for dinner. She went to the windows and opened the heavy wooden shutters, letting the outside air in. As she had in von Schmidt's castello, she sat curled up in the window seat and stared outside as she waited for Pierce. If there had been any hope for the two of them, it was gone now. After today, she'd be lucky if he'd pass her on the street without crossing to the other side. But she couldn't really regret anything she'd done, particularly now that Sidney's name was cleared.

She had no idea how much time had passed when the door finally opened. Pierce stood silhouetted by a hall light as he looked into the darkened room. "Samantha?"

She didn't rise. "I'm here, by the window."

Without turning on the light, he walked across the room and sat at the opposite end of the window seat.

"How's your arm?"

"A little sore, but fine. The bullet didn't hit anything important."

Relief flooded through her. "I'm glad."

"I assumed you would be," he said dryly.

Her quick smile flashed. "Stop it. I don't want to smile."

"Why not?"

"This is too serious. What's happened is all my fault."

"I told you earlier that I wasn't going to argue with you about that." He shook his head. "I thought I was going to have a heart attack when I saw you standing there with a bread stick in von Schmidt's back. A bread stick!"

"The waiter wasn't thrilled with me either."

"That's because you filched it from his table."

Samantha was quiet for a moment. "Why did you want me here when you came back?"

"We need to talk."

"No," she said softly, "we don't. I know what you're going to say and I'd rather not actually have to listen to it. I'd like to be able to leave here with a little of my dignity intact."

"What exactly is it that you think I'm going to say?"

"That your life has been one long nightmare ever since I came into it."

"I see. Go on."

Sam took a deep breath and pushed her hair away from her face. The lights from outside reflected on his face. She wanted to drop her eyes, but forced them to remain on his. "That the night we almost made love was a mistake. It was never your intention to get involved with me. I just sort of dragged you into my life whether you wanted to be there or not."

"Back up a minute. Why do you believe that I'd think that night was a mistake?"

"Because, despite your better judgment, you're a little fond of me. You were feeling very protective of me that night. Very close. I took advantage."

A corner of his mouth lifted. "You took advantage?"

"I've never made a secret of how I felt about you."

"No, you haven't," he agreed. "You couldn't have even if you'd wanted to. Everything you feel—everything you think—is in those beautiful eyes of yours."

Now she lowered those eyes. "I'd like to leave now."

"No."

She looked up again. "Why?"

"Because I want you here, with me."

"I don't understand."

"No, but I do finally." He started outside, leaving Sam looking at his profile. "I don't know how to explain myself to you, Samantha. I hardly know how to explain me to myself." He turned his head and met her gaze. "When I met you, I'd just made up my mind to marry Barbara. There wasn't what you'd call love on either side, but there was respect, and a certain mutual affection. As you may have noticed, Barbara is a very serene person. No ups. No downs. She's always somewhere in the middle. I thought that was what I wanted. And then I met you."

"And you didn't approve of me at all."

"I told myself I didn't. I mean there you were, in jail for picking a man's lock. Disapproval was easy. But there was something else. I didn't know what it was then. I fought against it and you. I wanted nothing to do with you, and yet I couldn't stay away. I didn't want to think about you, and yet I couldn't stop myself." He looked at her quietly. "When I realized that it was you who'd gone off that bridge—when I thought I'd lost you—" he shook his head, searching for the words "—it was as though something in me had died with you. I knew in that moment that without you, there was nothing left for me. I became meaningless. And then you were there, and it was as though you'd handed me my life back with your own."

"But you didn't say any of that."

"You were hardly in a condition to listen to my declarations of love at that point, and I was too busy trying to get you home and to a doctor in any event. I thought we'd have time later. But then you took off again."

"I expected to be rejected. I didn't want to go through that."

Pierce reached out and cupped her cheek. "For a woman who's as sensitive as you are, you can be remarkably dense. You should have known from the way I kissed you, from the way I touched you, that what was between us was far from over."

"I'm sorry."

He leaned forward and softly kissed her forehead and her eyelids, then brushed his mouth against hers. "I love you, Samantha English. More than I ever thought it possible to love anyone. And if you think I'm going to let you leave me now, when I've gone through all of this just to get you back, you're sadly, sadly mistaken." He tangled his fingers in his hair and raised his head as he looked at her. "You're going to marry me, and we'll worry about the rest later."

Samantha's eyes searched his, afraid to believe what was happening but unable to deny what she saw. "I'm going to be difficult to live with."

He rubbed his thumb over her mouth. "Probably."

"I want to keep doing what I'm doing."

"I expected as much."

"I want children."

"You'll make a delightful mother."

Samantha's throat closed with emotion, and she couldn't speak for a minute. She raised her hand to Pierce's face and softly trailed it over his beard-shadowed cheek. "I love you so much."

Pierce picked her up in his arms and carried her to the bed. He laid her gently down and remained leaning over her, looking into her eyes.

"What is it?" Sam asked.

He shook his head. "There are some things that can't be put into words." His mouth covered hers in a kiss that was long and deep. Then he straightened and smiled down at her. "Now, about those babies you mentioned earlier..."

* * * * *

*...and now an exciting short story
from Silhouette Books.*

*

HEATHER GRAHAM POZZESSERE

Shadows on the Nile

CHAPTER ONE

Alex could tell that the woman was very nervous.
Her fingers were wound tightly about the arm rests,
and she had been staring straight ahead since the flight
began. Who was she? Why was she flying alone? Why
to Egypt? She was a small woman, fine-boned, with
classical features and porcelain skin. Her hair was
golden blond, and she had blue-gray eyes that were
slightly tilted at the corners, giving her a sensual and
exotic appeal.

And she smelled divine. He had been sitting there,
glancing through the flight magazine, and her scent
had reached him, filling him like something rushing
through his bloodstream, and before he had looked at
her he had known that she would be beautiful.

John was frowning at him. His gaze clearly said that
this was not the time for Alex to become interested in
a woman. Alex lowered his head, grinning. Nuts to
John. He was the one who had made the reservations
so late that there was already another passenger between them in their row. Alex couldn't have remained
silent anyway; he was certain that he could ease the
flight for her. Besides, he had to know her name, had

to see if her eyes would turn silver when she smiled. Even though he should, he couldn't ignore her.

"Alex," John said warningly.

Maybe John was wrong, Alex thought. Maybe this was precisely the right time for him to get involved. A woman would be the perfect shield, in case anyone was interested in his business in Cairo.

The two men should have been sitting next to each other, Jillian decided. She didn't know why she had wound up sandwiched between the two of them, but she couldn't do a thing about it. Frankly, she was far too nervous to do much of anything.

"It's really not so bad," a voice said sympathetically. It came from her right. It was the younger of the two men, the one next to the window. "How about a drink? That might help."

Jillian took a deep, steadying breath, then managed to answer. "Yes...please. Thank you."

His fingers curled over hers. Long, very strong fingers, nicely tanned. She had noticed him when she had taken her seat—he was difficult not to notice. There was an arresting quality about him. He had a certain look: high-powered, confident, self-reliant. He was medium tall and medium built, with shoulders that nicely filled out his suit jacket, dark brown eyes, and sandy hair that seemed to defy any effort at combing it. And he had a wonderful voice, deep and compelling. It broke through her fear and actually soothed her. Or perhaps it was the warmth of his hand over hers that did it.

"Your first trip to Egypt?" he asked. She managed a brief nod, but was saved from having to comment when the stewardess came by. Her companion ordered her a white wine, then began to converse with her quite normally, as if unaware that her fear of flying had nearly rendered her speechless. He asked her what she did for a living, and she heard herself tell him that she was a music teacher at a junior college. He responded easily to everything she said, his voice warm and concerned each time he asked another question. She didn't think; she simply answered him, because flying had become easier the moment he touched her. She even told him that she was a widow, that her husband had been killed in a car accident four years ago, and that she was here now to fulfill a long-held dream, because she had always longed to see the pyramids, the Nile and all the ancient wonders Egypt held.

She had loved her husband, Alex thought, watching as pain briefly darkened her eyes. Her voice held a thread of sadness when she mentioned her husband's name. Out of nowhere, he wondered how it would feel to be loved by such a woman.

Alex noticed that even John was listening, commenting on things now and then. How interesting, Alex thought, looking across at his friend and associate.

The stewardess came with the wine. Alex took it for her, chatting casually with the woman as he paid. Charmer, Jillian thought ruefully. She flushed, realizing that it was his charm that had led her to tell him so much about her life.

Her fingers trembled when she took the wineglass. "I'm sorry," she murmured. "I don't really like to fly."

Alex—he had introduced himself as Alex, but without telling her his last name—laughed and said that was the understatement of the year. He pointed out the window to the clear blue sky—an omen of good things to come, he said—then assured her that the airline had an excellent safety record. His friend, the older man with the haggard, world-weary face, eventually introduced himself as John. He joked and tried to reassure her, too, and eventually their efforts paid off. Once she felt a little calmer, she offered to move, so they could converse without her in the way.

Alex tightened his fingers around hers, and she felt the startling warmth in his eyes. His gaze was appreciative and sensual, without being insulting. She felt a rush of sweet heat swirl within her, and she realized with surprise that it was excitement, that she was enjoying his company the way a woman enjoyed the company of a man who attracted her. She had thought she would never feel that way again.

"I wouldn't move for all the gold in ancient Egypt," he said with a grin, "and I doubt that John would, either." He touched her cheek. "I might lose track of you, and I don't even know your name."

"Jillian," she said, meeting his eyes. "Jillian Jacoby."

He repeated her name softly, as if to commit it to memory, then went on to talk about Cairo, the pyramids at Giza, the Valley of the Kings, and the beauty of the nights when the sun set over the desert in a riot of blazing red.

And then the plane was landing. To her amazement, the flight had ended. Once she was on solid ground again, Jillian realized that Alex knew all sorts of things about her, while she didn't know a thing about him or John—not even their full names.

They went through customs together. Jillian was immediately fascinated, in love with the colorful atmosphere of Cairo, and not at all dismayed by the waiting and the bureaucracy. When they finally reached the street she fell head over heels in love with the exotic land. The heat shimmered in the air, and taxi drivers in long burnooses lined up for fares. She could hear the soft singsong of their language, and she was thrilled to realize that the dream she had harbored for so long was finally coming true.

She didn't realize that two men had followed them from the airport to the street. Alex, however, did. He saw the men behind him, and his jaw tightened as he nodded to John to stay put and hurried after Jillian.

"Where are you staying?" he asked her.

"The Hilton," she told him, pleased at his interest. Maybe her dream was going to turn out to have some unexpected aspects.

He whistled for a taxi. Then, as the driver opened the door, Jillian looked up to find Alex staring at her. She felt...something. A fleeting magic raced along her spine, as if she knew what he was about to do. Knew, and should have protested, but couldn't.

Alex slipped his arm around her. One hand fell to her waist, the other cupped her nape, and he kissed her. His mouth was hot, his touch firm, persuasive. She was filled with heat; she trembled...and then she broke away at last, staring at him, the look in her eyes more eloquent than any words. Confused, she turned away and stepped into the taxi. As soon as she was seated she turned to stare after him, but he was already gone, a part of the crowd.

She touched her lips as the taxi sped toward the heart of the city. She shouldn't have allowed the kiss; she barely knew him. But she couldn't forget him.

She was still thinking about him when she reached the Hilton. She checked in quickly, but she was too late to acquire a guide for the day. The manager suggested that she stop by the Kahil bazaar, not far from the hotel. She dropped her bags in her room, then took another taxi to the bazaar. Once again she was enchanted. She loved everything: the noise, the people, the donkey carts that blocked the narrow streets, the shops with their beaded entryways and beautiful wares in silver and stone, copper and brass. Old men smoking water pipes sat on mats drinking tea, while younger men shouted out their wares from stalls and doorways. Jillian began walking slowly, trying to take it all in. She was occasionally jostled, but she kept her hand on her purse and sidestepped quickly. She was just congratulating herself on her competence when she was suddenly dragged into an alley by two Arabs swaddled in burnooses.

"What—" she gasped, but then her voice suddenly fled. The alley was empty and shadowed, and night was coming. One man had a scar on his cheek, and held a long, curved knife; the other carried a switchblade.

"Where is it?" the first demanded.

"Where is what?" she asked frantically.

The one with the scar compressed his lips grimly. He set his knife against her cheek, then stroked the flat side down to her throat. She could feel the deadly coolness of the steel blade.

"Where is it? Tell me now!"

Her knees were trembling, and she tried to find the breath to speak. Suddenly she noticed a shadow emerging from the darkness behind her attackers. She gasped, stunned, as the man drew nearer. It was Alex.

Alex . . . silent, stealthy, his features taut and grim.
Her heart seemed to stop. Had he come to her rescue?
Or was he allied with her attackers, there to threaten,
even destroy, her?

*   *   *   *   *

*Watch for Chapter Two of SHADOWS ON
THE NILE coming next month—only in
Silhouette Intimate Moments.*

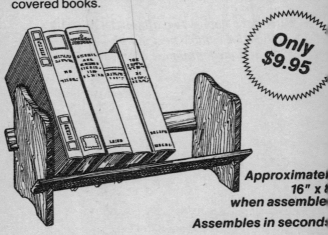

In response
to last year's outstanding success,
Silhouette Brings You:

Silhouette Christmas Stories 1987

Specially chosen for you in a delightful volume celebrating the holiday season, four original romantic stories written by four of your favorite Silhouette authors.

Dixie Browning—*Henry the Ninth*
Ginna Gray—*Season of Miracles*
Linda Howard—*Bluebird Winter*
Diana Palmer—*The Humbug Man*

Each of these bestselling authors will enchant you with their unforgettable stories, exuding the magic of Christmas and the wonder of falling in love.

A heartwarming Christmas gift during the holiday season...indulge yourself and give this book to a special friend!

Available November 1987

XM87-1